DYNASTIES

Seven Sins

One man's betrayal can destroy generations.

Fifteen years ago, a hedge-fund hotshot vanished with billions, leaving the high-powered families of Falling Brook changed forever.

Now seven heirs, shaped by his betrayal, must reckon with the sins of the past.

Passion may be their only path to redemption.

Experience all Seven Sins!

* * *

Ruthless Pride by **Naima Simone**

This CEO's pride led him to give up his dreams for his family. Now he's drawn to the woman who threatens everything...

Forbidden Lust by **Karen Booth**

He's always resisted his lust for his best friend's sister—until they're stranded together in paradise...

Insatiable Hunger by **Yahrah St. John**

His unbridled appetite for his closest friend is unleashed when he believes she's fallen for the wrong man...

Hidden Ambition by **Jules Bennett**

Ambition has taken him far, but revenge could cost him his one chance at love...

Reckless Envy by **Joss Wood**

When this shark in the boardroom meets the one woman he can't have, envy takes over...

Untamed Passion by **Cat Schield**

Will this black sheep's self-destructive wrath flame out when he's expecting an heir of his own?

Slow Burn by **Janice Maynard**

If he's really the idle playboy his family claims, will his inaction threaten a reunion with the woman who got away?

"I'm not with Hugh anymore. We're on a break."

Ryan's eyes darkened. "Why didn't you tell me?"

"Because we nearly kissed that night and it threw me for a loop. Just like tonight did. I couldn't continue seeing him if I had feelings for another man, so we broke up."

Ryan's gaze locked with hers, and then he drew her to him and as he pinned her against him, his mouth sought hers.

When he pulled away, he held both sides of her face and peered into her eyes. "Tell me to stop, Jessie, because I don't know if I can."

"I don't want you to stop, Ryan. I need you."

He leaned his forehead against hers, his lips a fraction away. "You're temptation for even the strongest man. You have no idea how much I want to make love to you."

She gasped and that very instant his mouth was back on hers.

* * *

Insatiable Hunger by Yahrah St. John
is part of the Dynasties: Seven Sins series.

YAHRAH ST. JOHN

INSATIABLE HUNGER

HARLEQUIN
DESIRE

Thank you to my agent Christine Witthohn for encouraging me to participate in the Seven Sins series.

Special thanks and acknowledgment are given to Yahrah St. John for her contribution to the Dynasties: Seven Sins miniseries.

DESIRE

Recycling programs
for this product may
not exist in your area.

ISBN-13: 978-1-335-20920-7

Insatiable Hunger

Copyright © 2020 by Harlequin Books S.A.

This edition published by arrangement with Harlequin Books S.A.

For questions and comments about the quality of this book, please contact us at CustomerService@Harlequin.com.

Harlequin Enterprises ULC
22 Adelaide St. West, 40th Floor
Toronto, Ontario M5H 4E3, Canada
www.Harlequin.com

Printed in U.S.A.

Dear Reader,

I'm thrilled to bring you the latest edition in the Seven Sins series. *Insatiable Hunger* delves into another Falling Brook couple whose lives were impacted by the fall of Black Crescent's hedge fund.

Jessie Acosta has put the pieces of her life back together after her family lost everything a decade ago because of a Ponzi scheme. She'd never looked at Ryan Hathaway, the boy next door, until their ten-year reunion, when a hunger surfaces for her sexy neighbor.

This isn't your everyday friends-to-lovers story—there's plenty of heat and passion between Jessie and Ryan, but there's also depth because Jessie has to overcome hidden family secrets, past loves, and being true to herself to find real and lasting love with Ryan.

Want to know more Yahrah St. John news? Visit my website, www.yahrahstjohn.com, and join my newsletter. Or feel free to write me at yahrah@yahrahstjohn.com.

Yours truly,

Yahrah St. John

Yahrah St. John is the author of thirty-two books and one deliciously sinful anthology. When she's not at home crafting one of her spicy romances with compelling heroes and feisty heroines with a dash of family drama, she is gourmet cooking or traveling the globe seeking out her next adventure. St. John is a member of Romance Writers of America. Visit www.yahrahstjohn.com for more information.

Books by Yahrah St. John

Harlequin Desire

The Stewart Heirs

At the CEO's Pleasure
His Marriage Demand
Red Carpet Redemption
The Stewart Heirs

Dynasties: Seven Sins

Insatiable Hunger

Harlequin Kimani Romance

Cappuccino Kisses
Taming Her Tycoon
Miami After Hours
Taming Her Billionaire
His San Diego Sweetheart

Visit her Author Profile page
at Harlequin.com for more titles.

You can also find Yahrah St. John on Facebook,
along with other Harlequin Desire authors,
at www.Facebook.com/harlequindesireauthors!

One

Falling Brook's country club had been given a face-lift, Jessie Acosta thought as she walked around the elegantly appointed ballroom. The Black & Silver Soirée theme was in full effect. Silver and black balloons hung from the ceiling and the tables were decked with black tablecloths and silver lamé runners.

Black and silver confetti had been sprinkled over the tables, giving them a festive touch, and on top of each sat either a glass vase filled with black tulips and silver-gray roses or a bowl topped with silver and black ornaments. Black plates sat atop silver chargers and held silver napkins and flatware. Reunion guests' names were in tiny silver frames next to each setting. The reunion committee had outdone itself.

Jessie herself had come prepared to dazzle in an

eye-catching, sequined spaghetti-strapped gown with a plunging V-neckline and an open back with crisscross detail. Or at least, that had been her intention, but her long-distance boyfriend, Hugh O'Malley, was nowhere to be found. When she'd asked him if he was coming home from London for the event, he'd informed her he was too busy at work. So she'd spent most of her evening in the company of Ryan Hathaway, at one time one of her oldest friends.

That changed fifteen years ago when her parents had lost their entire fortune because of Black Crescent Investments. CEO Vernon Lowell had embezzled millions from his clients—her parents included—disappearing before authorities could catch him. That loss had led Jessie to always wanting to make her parents happy and to do what was expected. Instead of hanging out with Ryan all the time, she'd started dating Hugh O'Malley, who was from one of the richest families in town, just to please them, and she knew they expected them to marry. But lately she'd become increasingly dissatisfied with the direction of her life and their long-distance relationship. And then tonight happened and suddenly she was seeing the world through a different lens.

Ryan stood a few feet away, talking to several of their classmates, but he was head and shoulders above them. Ryan wasn't the sweet, shy boy next door who wore glasses and was slightly overweight she'd grown up with. The Ryan Hathaway she'd met tonight was confident, lean and trim, and wore contacts. There wasn't anything shy about him. He was sexy and carried it well in a black custom-fit tuxedo.

Jessie hadn't be able to stop herself from ogling. It had been several years since she'd last seen him. Ryan's once-curly black hair had been cut into a close-cropped fade along the sides with curly tendrils at the top. And since when did he have facial hair? It was just a smattering—a mustache and fuzz on the chin—but it gave him a hint of mystery and danger. His charcoal eyes had been trained on her for most of the night and, to Jessie's surprise, she kind of liked it.

When they'd talked, it was like the years faded away and they were just Ryan and Jessie sitting in his tree house and talking about their dreams for the future. Ryan had done quite well for himself. He worked for a high-profile investment company in Manhattan while Jessie toiled away as an associate at a midsize firm in corporate law.

It amazed her that they'd been in the same city yet hardly seen each other. But how would they, when she worked sixty-hour weeks? Sometimes more. She wanted to make partner and the only way to do that was to get those billable hours.

"Penny for your thoughts?" Ryan asked, suddenly by her side. She'd been so engrossed in thought, she hadn't seen him wander over.

"Just thinking about how so much has changed," Jessie said, glancing up at him from underneath her lashes. "You, especially."

A large grin spread across his incredibly full lips. *Why hadn't she noticed how divine they were before?* "Me? I'm the same Ryan you've always known."

Jessie shook her head. "I beg to differ. You're different."

"Is that a bad thing?"

She smiled. "No, it's a *great* thing."

He regarded her silently for a moment, as if weighing his options. "Care to dance?"

"I would love to."

Any thoughts she had evaporated the moment Ryan pulled her against him. Jessie felt…well, sort of strange because they'd never danced together. Maybe when they were little and had been playing around. In his arms now, Jessie felt acutely aware of her body and the way her breasts crushed against Ryan's chest.

Raw masculine heat radiated from his close proximity, causing her heart to flutter uncontrollably. And when Ryan pressed his body against hers and slid his thigh between the softness of hers, Jessie nearly lost it. This was *Ryan*. It wasn't right she should be feeling these things…but she did.

He smelled so good. *Felt so good.* When he wound his arms around her waist, Jessie wanted to reach up on her tiptoes and sweep her lips across his. *What was wrong with her?* Ryan was her friend, but he didn't feel like a friend. She glanced up and peered into his eyes. He didn't look at her like one, either.

His ebony gaze raked over her face, his eyes trained on her mouth. He was going to kiss her. And she wanted him to. *Desperately.* She wanted to feel his lips crushed against her own, only then might it slake the hunger growing deep in her belly. She licked her lips in anticipation and watched Ryan's eyes grow dark with desire.

He wound his fingers through her shoulder-length bob, bringing her face to his.

"Ryan!"

"Tell me you don't want me to kiss you," he taunted.

Jessie opened her mouth to say no, but she couldn't get the word out. And it would be a lie because she did want Ryan's kiss. She closed her eyes, preparing herself for an unforgettable kiss, when suddenly there was commotion behind them.

Startled, Jessie glanced over Ryan's shoulder to see Hugh saunter into the ballroom amid much fanfare.

Hugh was her dream guy—all six feet of him. With his classic good looks, she'd been in love with him since she was a teenager. Wavy jet-black hair cut just above the neck, piercing blue eyes, a sculpted face and a square jaw encompassed by day-old stubble made Hugh O'Malley Falling Brook's hottest catch. He was the man she was supposed to marry.

The tailored white tuxedo he wore fit him handsomely, but he'd always looked good in a suit. The fact he was there was a big deal considering he hadn't been back to the States for months. Everyone at Falling Brook Prep had loved Hugh and she'd been no exception. *So why had she been falling over her onetime best friend?*

Jessie immediately pushed against Ryan's chest and stepped a few inches away.

"What is it?" he asked and then swiveled in the direction of her gaze. His expression turned from sexy and slumberous to irritated. Ryan glanced back at Jessie. "Now that Hugh is here, the party's over?"

"Ryan…"

He held up his hand. "It's okay. I was only a stand-in until the man you really wanted came along. If you'll excuse me…"

He didn't make it far because Hugh blocked his path. "Well, if it isn't Ryan Hathaway. How are you, man?"

"Fine."

Ryan tried to move past him but Hugh wasn't budging. Instead, he wrapped an arm around Jessie's shoulders. "Thanks for keeping my lady occupied until I could get here. My flight got delayed. It was a real bear traveling from London. How's my Jess?" He bent down and kissed her on the forehead.

Jessie glanced over at Ryan, who was fuming at her. "I'm…uh, good." She felt like a total heel to have her boyfriend in front of her when two seconds ago she'd been lusting after Ryan.

"I'm going to mingle." Ryan, not waiting for a response, made a hasty retreat.

Jessie watched him leave, feeling incredibly guilty for leading him on. If Hugh hadn't arrived…

"Never known you to be so tongue-tied, babe," Hugh responded, breaking into her thoughts.

Jessie blinked, refocusing on Hugh. "I'm shocked. I didn't know you were coming."

Hugh grinned broadly. "I wanted to surprise you. I know it's been tough the last few years with our long-distance relationship, so I was trying to make an effort."

Jessie forced a smile. "I appreciate that."

"Do you? Because I could do with a better greeting after not seeing each other for months." Hugh wrapped her in his embrace and planted a long kiss on Jessie's lips, but all she could think about was the anger etched on Ryan's features as he'd departed.

Would he ever learn? Ryan wondered as he stared at Hugh and Jessie from across the ballroom. Hugh was in his element with a crowd of their Falling Brook prepsters flocked around him, Jessie standing by his side like an adoring girlfriend.

Of course, she hadn't been so adoring moments before Hugh's arrival…

When he'd looked at her, Ryan had been entranced by the bow of her slightly parted mouth, by her slender throat and the gentle swell of her breasts. Jessie had made his breath catch and he hadn't been able to take his eyes off her. Warning bells should have sounded in his head the minute she'd looked at him the way a woman looked at a man—*him*—like she wanted him to kiss her. He'd taken full advantage of her desire for him, sweeping Jessie into his arms and showing her just how good they could be together. He knew what he wanted and it seemed Jessie had finally, truly, seen him.

Not as a friend.

But as a man.

A man she wanted.

Had he mistaken the signs that she was interested?

Surely not, Ryan wasn't a novice when it came to women. He'd read Jessie's body language. The way she'd leaned into him, pressed her small but firm breasts against him, which had caused him to nearly erupt.

Ryan had had a crush on Jessie since he was six years old when she'd moved to Sycamore Street with her parents and brother, Pete Jr. The Hathaways and Acostas had been close neighbors once. Their fathers had played golf at this very same country club, while their moms had volunteered at the prep school. Both families had often met up at soccer games to see Ryan's two older brothers, Ben and Sean, or Pete Jr. play soccer.

Meanwhile, Ryan and Jessie had shared an easy rapport, often spending hours in each other's company, hanging out at one of their homes playing video games or riding their bicycles to the town square for ice cream. But Jessie had never seen Ryan as anything other than a friend. The situation had only worsened after Black Crescent's hedge fund tanked, leaving the Acosta family as collateral damage in its wake. Adversity hadn't brought him and Jessie closer. Instead, they'd grown further apart.

"Are you all right, Ryan?" one of their classmates asked. "You look like you're ready to blow your lid."

Ryan inhaled deeply and schooled his expression. "Sorry. I was deep in thought about a deal I've got going."

"Are you sure?" the man inquired. "Because your deadly glare was aimed at Hugh over there." He inclined his head toward the man of the hour.

Everyone was fawning all over Hugh and, while Ryan hated to admit it, he was jealous. He had to let go of the notion that he and Jessie would ever *be* together. Time and time again, he'd watched her choose Hugh over him and tonight had been no different. He needed to move on with his life for good this time. The time for looking back on what might have been was gone.

"Yeah. I'm good," Ryan replied. "I'm going to cut out, it's been a long night and I've seen all I need to see." Ryan turned on his heel and walked out of the ballroom toward the valet. Regardless of the kiss he and Jessie almost shared, they were over. He wasn't willing to play second fiddle to any man and certainly not Hugh O'Malley. One day he would find the woman meant for him. She certainly wasn't in this ballroom.

"Babe, I'm so happy I came," Hugh said after the crowd surrounding them dissipated, leaving him and Jessie alone. He swept her into his arms, but when he bent to kiss her, Jessie turned her head to the side. His eyebrows shot up in surprise. "What's wrong?"

Her lips twisted in a cynical smile. "What's wrong? Really, Hugh? You didn't even tell me you were coming and I'm supposed to welcome you with open arms?"

His blue eyes regarded her warily. "Actually, yeah, that's what I thought. Excuse me if I thought you might be happy to see me."

Jessie sighed. She *should* be happy to see him, but her reaction to Ryan tonight was a problem. She turned away from Hugh and walked swiftly toward the covered terrace. The committee had bedecked it with string lights and balloons. Since the night air held a chill, heaters had been strategically placed around the terrace.

Hugh followed her, catching up in two quick strides, and spun her around. "Jessie, what's going on?"

"Nothing." She looked down at the floor.

"We may have been apart for a while, but I can tell when you have something on your mind. What is it?"

After almost kissing Ryan, Jessie realized she was done with playing the "perfect couple." She was tired of living up to everyone's expectations. She knew her parents thought they would get married; expected her to be the dutiful daughter she'd always been. But Jessie didn't think so. If she and Hugh were meant to be, there was no way Jessie would have had such an intense and passionate encounter with Ryan. She had to do the right thing and end their relationship.

"I can't do this."

"Do what?"

"Be with you," Jessie stated. "*We*. Aren't. Working. We haven't been for some time because you're across the ocean. Besides, you and I both know that we've been together mainly because of our parents' wishes, not because it's what we both want."

"I'm sorry, Jessie. I know I've been caught up in my career, but surely you don't mean what you're saying. I've worked so hard for us—to build a better future."

"Hugh, we haven't lived in the same place, let alone the same country, for years. How are we supposed to get married one day if we never spend any time with one another?"

Hugh ruffled his hands through his dark curls. "I can't leave my job right now. I've got major deals in the works. It would ruin everything I've been working toward."

"I know. Your career has always been more important than our relationship, which is why I think we need to break up."

"I see."

"Please tell me you understand," Jessie pleaded.

"I do. I haven't been there for you and now you're evaluating if you want to continue our relationship. But instead of breaking up, why don't we take a break and think about what we both really want?"

Jessie lowered her head and tears clouded her eyes. She'd always thought they would be together forever, but she wasn't so sure now, not after tonight with Ryan. She glanced up at him through wet lashes. "Yes."

"Oh, sweetheart." Hugh pulled her into his arms, cradling her underneath his chin. "It's all right, take all the time you need and I'll do the same. But know I'm rooting for us."

Jessie wished she could say the same, but the way she'd felt tonight with Ryan showed her she wasn't as all-in on Hugh as she'd once thought. Otherwise why had she been thinking about Ryan the way she had tonight? She'd also come to realize that her *own* happiness came first, not what her parents or the citizens of Falling Brook expected from her.

"Can we keep the break private?" Hugh asked, glancing down at her. "I don't want to make it public or tell our parents yet in case…" His voice trailed off.

Jessie understood. Hugh had always cared about what people thought of him—how he was perceived. She was sure he thought there was hope they would get back together. And why wouldn't he? They were Falling Brook Prep's golden couple. "Of course. It will stay between us."

They left the terrace and went back into the party, pretending to be the happy couple in front of their peers.

But deep down, Jessie knew it was over between them because tonight her eyes had been opened to not only stop living her life according to her parents' expectations, but finally to do what's right for herself.

Two

Three months later

"It's good to see you, Ryan," Jessie had said when he'd strode into the famous restaurant in lower Manhattan near the financial district. He'd unbuttoned his suit jacket and taken a seat across from her. Within minutes, they'd ordered and received their meals. They had little to talk about other than the weather.

Ryan hadn't seen Jessie since their ten-year high school reunion and had been surprised when, out of the blue, she'd asked him to lunch. With her busy career, Ryan had assumed she hardly gave lunch a thought, while he, on the other hand, believed in eating small meals throughout the day. He supposed it had something to do with being overweight as a preteen and the endless bullying he'd received. He now religiously watched his weight, which was why he was eating a grilled salmon and spinach salad at the exclusive eatery.

Ryan sipped his club soda. "I was pleasantly surprised to get the invite."

Jessie released a long sigh. "You shouldn't be. We were close once."

"That was a long time ago, Jessie."

"And I'd like to rectify that," she stated.

Ryan peered into her earnest eyes and, damn him, he believed her.

Hadn't he told himself he was saying goodbye to the decades-old crush he'd had on this woman since his voice had begun to change?

He steepled his fingers together on the table. "I'm listening…" He measured his response. He wasn't about to rush to judgment. This could be nothing more than loneliness in the big city. Perhaps Jessie was in need of a dose of the familiar?

"Did you see the newspaper's fifteenth-anniversary article about Black Crescent?"

He was right. Jessie wanted a shoulder to cry on or someone to listen. In the past, he'd been all too willing to give an ear. Except this time, it was different. He wasn't the young, naïve teenager he'd once been, hoping for a scrap of her time. He was done with wishing and hoping Jessie would see him differently. He was a grown man and he had plenty of women he could call who were eager to spend time with him. "Yes. It's the same ole, same ole, Jessie. Why get rattled?"

"It may be old news to you, but not to my family,"

Jessie replied, dismay in her tone. "My father has never gotten over Black Crescent's hedge fund tanking. When Vernon Lowell disappeared, my father lost his job, his friends and his country-club membership. He nearly lost the house, too, but somehow Mama was able to hang on to it."

Ryan heard the wounded tone in her voice. He, too, had always wondered how the Acostas had managed to stay in their five-bedroom house when many of the other Falling Brook scions had fallen. He doubted Mrs. Acosta could have been making much in her receptionist job at O'Malley Luxury Motors, Hugh's father's company. "I'm glad your parents were able to keep the house. Otherwise, you and I wouldn't have remained friends."

Jessie pursed her lips. "Yeah, but it was never the same, was it? I know I pulled away from our friendship."

Ryan was shocked Jessie was owning up to it. As the years had gone by, he'd watched their relationship steadily fade into a shadow of its former self. "Why did you?"

Jessie was silent for several moments, then reached for her water glass, sipping generously. "When I learned that Jack O'Malley paid for Pete's and my tuition at Falling Brook Prep, I felt like I owed them my loyalty, you know? How could I forget what he'd done? Because of him, we were able to stay at prep school when most of our classmates had to withdraw and enroll in public school."

"I can understand your need to show your appreciation, but it didn't stop there, Jessie, and we both know why."

She arched a brow. "What do you have against Hugh?"

"Hugh? I don't want to talk about him." Ryan's mouth clenched tightly. "We were talking about Black Crescent and the impact it had not only on your family but our friendship."

Jessie took the bait and stopped talking about his rival. "That exposé brought to the surface all those old wounds. My mother said my father was beside himself after reading it and refused to come out of his study for the rest of the day. And then Joshua Lowell had that press conference to announce he was stepping down as CEO to live happily-ever-after. How dare he! He shouldn't get a happy ending after what his family did to the rest of us."

"I'm sorry to hear that about your dad," Ryan said. "Truly I am. And I get that Black Crescent has a black stain in your book. But what if someone could come along to revitalize it with fresh ideas to make the company better, more transparent?"

Jessie stared at him with a dumbfounded expression. "Why do you sound like a walking interviewee?"

Ryan took a forkful of salad and focused on chewing his food. This was a conversation he was not looking forward to. He'd known one day it would come, but it had come sooner than he liked.

Jessie's eyes grew large with expectation. "Well?"

"I've interviewed for the CEO position at Black Crescent. When Joshua Lowell made a formal announcement that he was stepping down to focus on his art career, that he'd gotten engaged and was currently in search for a successor, I tossed my hat into the ring."

"You've done what?" Her raised voice caused several patrons to openly stare in their direction.

Ryan wiped his mouth with his napkin. "Can you lower your voice, please?"

"I can't," she hissed. "You're making the worst mistake of your life! How can you even consider working for the family—the company—that destroyed mine? I thought we were friends."

"We are."

"Then how can you do this?"

Ryan reached across the table for Jessie's hand, but she shrank back in her chair, away from him. He took that one on the chin. He knew his announcement would come as a shock to her, but the position had also been a way for him to cut off feelings for her full-stop. He knew that working at Black Crescent, the company Jessie despised, was a surefire way to keep her away. She blamed Black Crescent for all her family's financial troubles and her father's inability to move forward with his life.

Her beautiful face was flushed bright red. "Why does it have to be you?"

"With my MBA and background, I'm uniquely qualified to take on the role. Who better to repair Black Crescent's damaged reputation?"

"Not you. When I spoke to Hugh, he thought—"

Ryan interrupted her, cutting off her sentence. "Wait just a minute. Hugh…hasn't been in Falling Brook in years. What would he know about the company?"

"He called me when Jack told him about the press conference."

When Ryan rolled his eyes, she pointed her index finger at him. "There it is."

"What is?"

"The animosity you always have whenever I bring up Hugh. Why do you dislike him so much?"

"I couldn't care less about Hugh," Ryan replied. "But you? You're giving this guy, who's been MIA for years, too much credit. I mean, how well do you even know him? When was the last time you spent any significant amount of time with the man?"

Was he pushing Jessie to admit her relationship with Hugh was a sham because he hadn't truly gotten over her? He'd stubbornly forced himself to forget about the almost kiss they'd shared at the reunion, but sitting across from Jessie now reminded him of how strong the attraction between them still was.

Jessie stared at Ryan in disbelief. The Ryan she remembered was always quiet, shy and even-keeled, yet the man sitting in front of her was anything but. In fact, she would say he was the opposite. He was confident with lots of swagger.

When he'd walked into the restaurant, Jessie had forced herself not to wag her tongue in delight. He'd looked resplendent in a gray suit, white shirt and skinny silver-striped tie, just as he had three months ago when she'd seen him at the ten-year reunion. She'd thought the heady, powerful feelings he'd evoked in her when they'd danced together had been a fluke.

A flare of heat had sparked within her on the dance floor, warming her in a way that surprised the heck out of her. If Hugh hadn't interrupted when he had, Jessie was certain Ryan would have kissed her and she would have liked it. That had been the most confounding thing of all. The unexpected desire she'd felt for her old friend.

So she'd pushed it down, spending the last few months purging her heightened emotions by working tirelessly at the law firm until well after dark. She'd tried convincing herself she'd imagined it, but she hadn't. The flame was there now, burning as bright as it had that night.

"Are you going to answer me?" Ryan asked, breaking into her thoughts. She saw the faintest clench of his jaw as his eyes narrowed at her. "Or can you not recall the last time you saw the great Hugh O'Malley? Was it the reunion? If so, that was months ago."

His tone brought Jessie out of her musings. "My relationship with Hugh is my business."

"You made it mine when you brought him into the conversation to pass along his advice. And I'm calling a spade a spade. You've been with the man on and off for years. Mostly off, in my opinion. Yet the consensus has always been that you're going to marry the guy. I'm pointing out that you might not know him enough to make such a monumental decision."

She knew that. It was why she'd agreed with Hugh to take a break. They'd texted frequently or FaceTimed and Skyped as often as they could for much of their relationship. And while Hugh attended Harvard and Wharton, they'd been able to maintain some semblance of being a couple, but it had been difficult with their demanding studies. However, when Hugh had decided to accept a job in London, straight out of Wharton, Jessie had been taken aback.

She'd thought Hugh would want to be closer, not farther apart. He'd insisted their relationship was strong enough to handle the distance and time apart. It hadn't been. Instead, Jessie had begun to feel restless, as if the life she'd carved out for herself was no longer enough. So she'd pushed herself harder at work, but that hadn't brought her the fulfillment she'd thought it would. She needed more.

"I admit marriage is a huge step," Jessie finally responded, "And we are not there yet." She had no idea where her relationship with Hugh stood at the moment. She didn't appreciate Ryan shining a light on it. "But, Hugh is a stand-up guy and the O'Malleys are good people."

"So you would marry him for his family? Because you feel obligated?"

"Of course not," she huffed. Though sometimes she felt that way, she couldn't tell Ryan that. "You're purposely misunderstanding me."

"Am I? Do you even know what you really want?"

Jessie narrowed her eyes. "Of course I do. There's no rush to jump into marriage. Hugh and I are focusing on our careers right now. It's been hard for me as an associate at my firm. I have to prove myself. It's the same for Hugh. We both have big dreams."

"Which is keeping you both on different continents. Sounds romantic."

"Don't presume to judge me, Ryan, when you don't have a relationship yourself."

"You don't know that," he countered.

Jessie stared into his dark brown eyes. Was he trying to get under her skin? Because if he was, it was working. Her nerves were frazzled imagining Ryan with someone else. Was it because she wanted him for herself? Her mind burned with visions of Ryan and another woman in an intimate embrace and she rapidly blinked to rid herself of the damning images. "Are you dating someone?"

He was silent for several beats before saying, "Not at the moment. But that's not to say I haven't enjoyed an active dating life. I've had girlfriends."

Girlfriends. Plural. "Bully for you."

Had she imagined Ryan was sitting home alone on the couch in front of the television waiting for her to acknowledge him? If so, she'd been wrong. He was a good-looking man and clearly finding someone to spend time with hadn't been a problem for him.

"Why should you care, Jessie? We're just friends, after all."

Jessie offered a bland smile even though she felt quite the opposite. She hadn't thought about Ryan like a friend since reunion night. "That's right. I want you to be happy."

"Good, then accept that I know what's best for me," Ryan stated. "And the opportunity to run Black Crescent and clean up its image is what I want."

Jessie frowned. "Are we back to that?"

"We never left."

Her eyes found his and his stare was uncompromising. He was digging in his heels. She sucked in a long-drawn breath. "I guess you can do whatever you want, but I can't support you on this, Ryan. It goes against everything I believe and against my family."

"I understand. Just don't fight me."

She chuckled. "Now you're asking too much. Fighting with you is one of my favorite pastimes." When they'd been younger, she would often give him the business to get a rise out of him.

"How about we stop fighting and have some fun?"

Jessie was surprised Ryan still wanted a relationship with her. Since the night of the reunion, he'd kept his distance. She suspected this potential job with Black Crescent was a way for him to create further distance between them. But until the reunion, she hadn't realized how much she'd missed him the past couple of years and the open camaraderie they'd always shared.

"Did you have something in mind?" she asked.

He grinned and her stomach knotted with a peculiar twisting motion. "Actually, I do. You remember my friend Adam?" She nodded, the name sounded familiar. "Well, with July Fourth coming up, he's invited a bunch of friends to his place in the Hamptons for the weekend. Would you be interested in going?"

"I would. You're sure he wouldn't mind you bringing a plus one? I haven't been to the beach all season. The city is so hot this time of year." Her roommate and bestie, Becca Edwards, had been trying to get Jessie to the beach, but she was usually working late, clocking in hours at her firm.

"Excellent. If you can get off early, I'll pick you up on Friday afternoon. Sound good?"

"I'm in," she told him. Despite knowing she was putting herself in the path of danger by going to the beach with Ryan for the weekend, she thought that, perhaps, she could put their relationship back into the box it had always been in. She would finally be able to stamp out his face, which had found itself floating into her dreams, both day and night.

She would do it.

She had to.

Although she was restless and dissatisfied with her life, she wasn't about to blow up her relationship with a dear friend over an attraction that would fade. Plus, if Ryan was considering a job at Black Crescent, it would be the antithesis of what her parents would want. She had to stay the course.

Figures danced on the screen in front of Ryan's eyes later that afternoon. He'd been staring at them for the last hour with little result of producing the report he'd wanted to complete by end of day. Leaning back in his executive chair, he glanced out the window from the forty-fourth floor of his office building.

Since his lunch with Jessie, he'd been out of sorts and unable to focus. At first, he'd thought it was because he'd finally spilled the beans about his job opportunity with Black Crescent, but that wasn't it at all.

It was Jessie. He'd thought going to lunch and telling her of his opportunity at Black Crescent would put a nail in the coffin of their already strained relationship. Instead, there was an awareness between them that hadn't been there before. When he'd peered into her beautiful brown eyes, he'd forgotten she was the next-door neighbor he'd known for nearly twenty years.

Instead, he was seeing a full-grown, woman with a wavy mass of thick black hair and a wide, generous mouth. And when her two dark orbs gazed on him, all Ryan had wanted to do was to sweep her into his arms and forget about everyone and everything. But he hadn't. This was Jessie. His friend.

Or was she?

Ryan had studied her during lunch, looking for signs Jessie felt the same vibes, and, if he wasn't mistaken, she had. There had definitely been a spark of electricity between them that'd had nothing to do with a dazzling evening underneath the stars. Ryan thought he'd ended that attraction. Pursuing the position with Black Crescent should have ensured any fantasy of being with Jessie was crushed, but the spark was still there.

Unfortunately, the attraction he'd felt for Jessie had become like an infection. One he was sure he could get rid of. He mustn't forget that Jessie had ignored him for years by choosing to be with Hugh and his family instead.

He squeezed his eyes shut trying to block out her image. If only he could block her out of his heart.

He hadn't lied when he'd told her he'd had girlfriends. Although the number was small—he was selective in the women he chose to go to bed with—he'd had lovers. None of which held a candle to Jessie, the woman he'd measured them all against. His last girl-friend had told him in no uncertain terms that until he dealt with his unrequited feelings for Jessie, he'd never truly move on with anyone.

Is that why he'd blurted out an invite to Adam's Hampton house? *Was he testing himself? Jessie?* To see if her relationship with Hugh as solid as she portrayed? To see if what they'd felt for each other on the dance floor was real or imagined?

And if he was testing, what result would the weekend produce?

Ryan supposed he would have to wait and see.

So why am I so excited at the prospect of finding out?

Three

"You're not coming home this weekend?" Angela Acosta asked when her daughter called her late in the evening from her office. Jessie was working late, as she always did, and apparently had only stopped to order some sushi for dinner.

"No, Mama. I have plans."

"But's it's July Fourth. I'd planned to have a big family BBQ. Your brother Pete is coming with his girlfriend, Amanda." Jessie could hear the pout in her mother's voice. "Surely, the firm can allow you to take some time off. You're working your fingers to the bone."

"I do have the long weekend off."

"Then why aren't you coming?"

"I have plans," Jessie stated.

"More important than your family?" her mother inquired.

Jessie didn't appreciate the guilt trip her mother was trying to lay on her. She was a dutiful daughter and came home more often than her big brother, so why was she being made to feel bad because she was taking time for herself? Plus, she wasn't too eager for a repeat performance of her last visit. When the Black Crescent article had come out, her father's mood had bottomed out, to say the least. Jessie had been dreading going home and this last-minute invitation for the weekend had provided the perfect excuse.

"I had these plans before I knew you had something planned," Jessie said. "I'm going to the beach with Ryan and some friends."

"Ryan from next door? What about Hugh?"

"What about him?"

"It's not right that you should be off gallivanting with another man when your fiancé is in another country."

"We're not engaged, Mama."

"But that's always been the plan—that you would get married."

"One day."

"Sounds more like no day," Angela said underneath her breath, but Jessie had heard her. And her mother had cause to be concerned. Jessie and Hugh were in trouble. If her weekend with Ryan took a turn, a permanent break might happen sooner than expected.

"Give Daddy my best," Jessie said, quickly rushing off the phone. She didn't want to feel guilty about spending time with Ryan. They were friends. But would they stay that way? She hadn't been able to forget how she'd felt when they'd danced, how her body responded in ways she could only contribute to its awareness of Ryan. His enticing scent had intoxicated her and she recalled feeling as if all the oxygen had been sucked out of her lungs. Her mind was telling her to follow the path she'd chosen, but her body was reminding her how completely dissatisfied she'd been over the years.

Jessie was curious. If they were alone again would she feel the same way?

The more important question is, if I do, will I explore those feelings?

"Do you really think it's a good idea to play with fire where Jessie's concerned?" Adam McKinley asked when Ryan told him he was bringing Jessie with him to the Hamptons for the weekend.

After settling down with a beer, Ryan had called his best friend once he'd finally made it home from work. "I'm not."

"Who do you think you're talking to?" Adam said on the other end of the line. "I'm the guy who listened to your sob story for years about how this girl never paid an ounce of attention to you. Who pretty much abandoned your friendship after her rich boyfriend's parents paid her high school tuition. Do you recall those conversations?"

"Of course I do." How could Ryan forget? He sounded pathetic. Like a real schmuck, hung up on a girl who paid him no mind. He wasn't that man anymore. "That's not what's happening here."

"Then you're lying to yourself," Adam stated bluntly. "You can't tell me there isn't some part of you hoping this weekend goes differently."

Ryan both hated and appreciated Adam's forthrightness. He was straddling the fence, so he spoke plainly. "I admit I've always wanted Jessie to see me in a different light. Not as a shoulder to cry or lean on, but as a man."

"And if she doesn't? I thought, after the reunion, you were done with wishing and hoping she would see you differently?"

"I was. Hugh came in and Jessie morphed right in front of me, but maybe away from our normal surroundings, she can be free to be herself."

"Free to be with you?"

"Yes."

Adam sighed. "All right, but don't say I didn't warn you."

Seconds later, Ryan looked at the phone in his hand. Spending the weekend with Jessie was a gamble, but it would enable him to see if the sparks he'd felt weren't one-sided.

It was totally worth risking their twenty-year friendship.

"You realize you've been trying to pack a weekend bag for over an hour," Becca told Jessie as she stared at the pile of clothes on her bed in their two-bedroom apartment in Chelsea when Thursday evening rolled around.

"I know, I know." Jessie sighed heavily. She had left the law firm around 7:00 p.m.—a reasonable hour given she usually stayed until nine, sometimes ten, o'clock—so she could go home to pack for her weekend with Ryan. But it wasn't a weekend with Ryan, per se. It was more like two friends hanging out together. So why was she stressing out over what outfits to bring?

"Then what's the problem?" Becca asked, her eyes glinting with amusement. "I mean you're going with Ryan. I thought you guys were just friends?"

"We are." Jessie lied.

"Are you sure about that?" Becca, sitting on Jessie's bed, looked up at her. "I've never seen you act this way except when you were fretting about Hugh coming for a visit."

Hugh.

Truth be told, Jessie hadn't thought about him in weeks other than when he'd called her about the Black Crescent press conference. And when he'd tried to Skype last night, she'd avoided the call. Pushing the clothes aside, Jessie joined Becca on the bed. "Can I be honest?"

"If you can't be honest with your roomie and friend of nearly a decade, who can you?"

Jessie smiled at the lovable redhead with the brilliant green eyes. Becca had been her roommate since her freshman year at NYU. When they'd met, they'd hit it off instantly. There'd been none of the craziness she might have assumed based on Becca's hair color. Instead, they were like sisters, often trading clothes because they were both a size four. They'd lived together ever since. Becca was a fashion buyer for Bloomingdales and often came home with great finds.

"I've been struggling with some unexpected feelings that have come up with Ryan."

"Did something happen?" Becca asked.

"Not really. Nothing concrete. Except…at our ten-year reunion at Falling Brook a few months back, something changed between us."

"You mean you finally noticed how drop-dead gorgeous he is?"

Jessie stared into Becca's green eyes. "What are you talking about?"

"C'mon, Jessie. You seem to be the only one oblivious to how good-looking Ryan is," Becca replied with a smirk. "Don't you remember how all the girls in the dorm went crazy whenever he came to visit?"

"Really?"

Becca chuckled. "Maybe not. You were too busy making goo-goo eyes at Hugh to notice, but Ryan is quite a catch. And now that he's working at that big investment company, some woman is going to come and snatch him up at any moment. So, if you're just noticing him, you've had your head in the sand. Now is as good a time as any to make your move."

"Becca!"

"I know I mentioned Hugh, but let's be real. You guys have had a long-distance relationship for nearly a decade. You both haven't lived in the same city since you were at prep school. Maybe it's time to let him go and start looking at all your options, including Ryan, who's been right in front of your face this entire time."

"That's not why I'm going to the Hamptons."

Becca raised a brow. "Aren't you?" She motioned to

all the strewed clothes on the bed. "The reason you're having such a hard time packing is because you're nervous. You want Ryan to like everything you're in. Or out of." She winked.

Becca was right in that Jessie wanted Ryan to find her attractive. *But did she want more?*

Maybe.

Ryan had invaded her dreams lately and she'd wondered how he'd looked outside of his clothes. The once chubby preteen she'd grown up with had thrown off the baby fat and was lean and trim. And very dangerous to her sensibilities.

Jessie stood. "Help me, then. I need to look my best." There was so much still unsettled. What if Ryan went to work for Black Crescent—the company that had caused her family so much pain and misfortune? And what about her own growing dissatisfaction with her life and wanting to step away from her parents and doing the expected? This weekend would surely be a test to see if she could break out of the mold of her life and embrace all life had to offer.

Ryan leaned against his Porsche 911 Carrera in front of Jessie's brownstone. It was a warm Friday afternoon in early July and, after working half a day, Ryan had returned home to change into a polo shirt and lightweight slacks for the trip to the Hamptons. Now he was waiting for Jessie to come down.

When the door opened to her building, it had been worth the wait. Instead of straightening her hair, Jessie had it in soft waves to her shoulders. She wore a pretty, yellow sundress with flowers all over it, showing off her olive skin.

He met her halfway up the steps and took her bag from her.

"Thanks." She smiled at him and his heart kicked over in his chest.

"No problem."

She glanced at his wheels and back up at him. "I like fast cars. How fast can it go?" she asked, following him to the back of the vehicle while he put her bag in the trunk.

"About 190 miles per hour."

Jessie grinned. "Then I can't wait for our two-hour drive to the Hamptons."

She didn't know the half of it, Ryan thought as he helped her into the vehicle. With the car so low to the ground, he watched Jessie try to climb in without showing too much skin. He closed the door behind her, but not after seeing a nice length of her smooth olive-toned legs.

When he climbed in, he looked over at her. "We aren't driving all the way there."

Jessie's brow furrowed. "Then how are we going to get there? Please tell me we are not taking the shuttle. If we are, I would have worn a more comfortable ensemble."

Ryan chuckled. "We are not taking a shuttle, either."

"Then how are getting there?"

"Helicopter."

Jessie's eyes narrowed as she regarded him. "So, you've been holding out on me."

"What do you mean?"

She eyed him warily. "You've always made it seem like your job was on the low end, yet you drive a Porsche and we're on our way to a helicopter?"

"Your point?"

"How wealthy are you?"

"It's indelicate to ask someone, Jessie," Ryan reprimanded, but he grinned at her. "But to answer your question, I do all right." He was more than all right, having already amassed his first million years ago, but he'd always held off bragging about his successes because he'd wanted to spare Jessie's feelings. He knew how hard it was for her and her parents to scrape by. He'd never wanted to flaunt his wealth.

"Clearly, it's more than that, while I will forever be mired in debt trying to pay off my student loan from law school."

"You'll get there," Ryan said, glancing quickly in her direction before returning his eyes to the road. "I know your work ethic. Failure is not an option for you."

"No, it's not," Jessie responded. "After seeing what happened to my father, I've always been determined to succeed at all costs. And once I make partner, my plan has always been to help my parents."

"And you will. I believe in you."

Jessie smiled and it lit up her entire face. "You always have. And I don't think I've ever told you, thank you."

"For what?"

"For your support. For your friendship. For never giving up on me when maybe I deserved it."

"You're being too hard on yourself. You deserve the best and then some."

They were silent for the remainder of the short ride to the Downtown Manhattan Heliport. After parking his Porsche 911 Carrera, he handed the keys to a gentleman wearing a polo shirt with the Porsche logo. He appeared to have been expecting him.

"What's going on?" she asked Ryan.

"They're going to service the car while I'm away and drop it back at my penthouse in Murray Hill. C'mon." Ryan picked up their bags and guided Jessie across the short distance to the helipad, where a bright red helicopter was waiting to take them to Adam's East Hampton beach house.

Jessie positively buzzed with excitement by his side. "Have you never been on one of these?" Ryan asked with amusement.

She shook her head.

"You've lived in Manhattan for nearly a decade."

"I know, but I've been too busy at the firm to have much time for extracurricular activities."

Ryan spoke with the pilot and, following the taking of several pictures that Jessie just had to have, their bags were loaded and they were ushered inside. After being given earphones so they could talk to each other, the helicopter soared into the air above the Manhattan skyline.

"It's stunning," Jessie said from beside him as they made a sweep around the city and got a view of the Empire State building and 911 Memorial. Soon, they were passing the Statue of Liberty and headed toward the Hamptons in Long Island. Ryan was excited for the weekend ahead and never more so when Jessie reached for his hand and gave it a squeeze.

"Thank you so much for this special treat." Her eyes were brimming with tears. "This is amazing!"

"You're welcome."

They landed at the Southampton Heliport located on the western end of the Meadow Lane peninsula in thirty minutes after taking off from Manhattan.

"I can't believe we flew here," Jessie said once they'd landed and taken off their earphones. "I feel like one of the rich and famous traveling to one of our summer homes."

"Glad I could oblige," Ryan said once he'd hopped out. Given she was wearing a dress and it was quite windy out, Ryan offered his hand so Jessie could hold onto her dress and avoid becoming Marilyn Monroe.

Unfortunately, she lost her footing. But Ryan was there to catch her. His heart raced triple-time as he held her in his arms. When she looked up at him, all Ryan thought about was kissing her pink and delectable lips, but he didn't go for it.

He'd promised himself three months ago that he was done waiting for her to come around to see that *he* was the man for her. One way or another, this weekend would either turn out to be a torture for him to stay away or a temptation he couldn't deny. Regardless, in the end, he would find out where he stood with Jessie.

Four

"Uh, thank you." Jessie's words came out in short, ragged pants. She could hardly think with the feel of Ryan's muscular body pressed so tightly against her own. It made her want to feel all of him. Squeezing her eyes shut, she counted to ten and then slowly disengaged herself. "I didn't realize 'knight in shining armor' was on your résumé."

She tried to make light of the sexual tension coming off Ryan in droves. Jessie was certain if she hadn't pulled away, he would have kissed her.

"Just one of many skills I have you're not privy to."

"Perhaps I'll learn more of them this weekend?" she purred.

Ryan grinned and Jessie realized she was flirting

with him. Her *friend*. It seemed strange, yet crazy, sexy cool at the same time.

"Our ride is here." Ryan indicated the black SUV parked nearby, its door being held open. "After you."

Jessie moved toward the vehicle, marveling at how Ryan managed to afford all of this. She'd underestimated how successful he was. Ryan didn't automatically brag to make himself look better, unlike Hugh, who was always quick to tell her about his latest deal and how much money he made. Jessie knew she shouldn't compare the two men, but they were the most important people in her life other than her family.

Speaking of family, she reached inside her purse and shot off a quick text to her mother, advising she'd arrived safely. The next was to Becca, along with a picture of them in front of the helicopter with the line, "Our ride to the Hamptons."

Becca was going to be green with envy.

"Everything okay?" Ryan asked from his side in the SUV.

"Oh, yes." Jessie put her phone away. "I was letting everyone know we arrived. My mother isn't too happy with me."

"Why?"

"Because I'm not spending the holiday weekend with them."

"Oh, I'm sorry. I should have realized. I know you don't get to go home often when you work so hard."

"Do you?"

"Oh, I do," Ryan chuckled. "But probably not nearly as much as I should. There's something about sleeping in your old room with all your teenage posters that feels kind of wrong."

"Your parents haven't changed it?"

He laughed. "No, and I've no idea why. Maybe Mom thinks if she keeps them long enough, my brothers and I will revert back to children."

"I miss your mom," Jessie said. Marilyn Hathaway was an amazing woman. Jessie had always looked up to her because, not only was she a principal, but a mother of three boys. Mrs. Hathaway made the "being a working mother thing" look easy and had convinced Jessie that one day she, too, could have it all.

"You know you can call her or stop by anytime. Mom has an open-door policy."

"Thank you. I might have to do that."

"Here we are," Ryan said as the SUV drove up a cul-de-sac to the wide gravel driveway of a big, classic, shingle-sided home with a large wraparound front porch. Several cars were already parked on the drive, she noticed as Ryan exited first and helped her out.

Seconds later, the grand front door opened almost instantaneously and a tall man with dark hair and a wide smile, wearing board shorts and a Columbia University T-shirt, wrapped Ryan in a big hug. Jessie remembered Adam; he'd been Ryan's roommate in college. But given they'd been at separate universities, her and Adam's paths hadn't crossed much. Jessie regretted that. "It's good to see you, man," Adam said to Ryan.

"You, too," Ryan returned. "You remember Jessie."

Adam walked toward her with open arms and gathered her in a hug. "Jessie, it's good to see you again. Glad you could make it to my humble abode."

"Welcome!" said a gorgeous brunette as she bounced down the steps to join them. She had to be nearly six feet, matching Adam in height, and was wearing a bikini top and cut-off jean shorts. She had long, flowing, dark brown hair that Jessie would kill for. "Name's Tia."

Jessie accepted her hand for a shake. "Pleasure to meet you."

"Let's show our guests where they'll be staying, honey." She looked at Adam. "Then a refreshment after traveling."

"I would love a drink," Ryan stated, but Jessie wasn't so sure. Something told her she was going to need to stay on her toes.

"There's only one bedroom?" Jessie asked.

After the McKinleys had given them a tour of the house with its double-height foyer, dark polished-wood floors, white interior with moldings, bright, open floor plan with views of the beach, and a chef's kitchen, they'd led them up the grand staircase to a palatial guest suite with a coffered ceiling. The king-size bed was turquoise and white with starfish and a white shag rag.

"Yes, I'm sorry." Tia shrugged. "I assumed when Ryan said he was bringing a friend that you were 'together.'"

She saw Ryan glare at Adam. "Adam, a word outside."

"I hope this won't be a problem." Tia glanced at her husband's retreating figure and then at Jessie. "I mean…

if you guys are platonic, I'm sure Ryan won't mind sleeping on the couch."

"We're friends," Jessie responded.

"Really?" Tia raised a brow. At Jessie's nod, she amended, "Why can't you share a bed?"

Because Jessie was having a hard time keeping her hands to herself. *How was she supposed to do that if the object of her affection was lying a few inches away?*

"Adam!" Ryan yelled as he followed his friend downstairs to the kitchen where Adam was headed for a slew of alcoholic beverages on the counter.

"What would you like?" Adam asked, ignoring Ryan's foul mood. "I've got vodka, rum, tequila and a darn good brandy I got from my dad last Christmas after I secured a big deal at the company."

"Are you going to ignore the elephant in the room?" Ryan knew his friend wasn't dense. "You knew Jessie and I would need two rooms. Yet you deliberately put us in one."

Adam pointed his index finger at Ryan. "Don't look at me like that. I didn't do it on purpose. Tia wanted to invite another couple, so I figured since the two of you are—" he used his fingers to make quotation marks "—just friends, there really wouldn't be an issue. You told me you were done."

Ryan turned to make sure no one was listening and moved closer. "I am, but I don't need the added temptation of sharing a bed with her."

"And I'm sorry," Adam said with a devilish grin, "but

all the rooms in the inn are full, my friend. You're just going to have to suck it up."

Ryan punched a fist into his hand and moved toward Adam.

Adam backed away. "Hey, look at it this way. I'm helping your cause. The close quarters will help you determine if you really are done with Jessie as you claim."

Ryan would have preferred not to chance his luck, but he was out of options. "Fix me a brandy, will you? I think I'm in for a bumpy weekend."

Ryan stayed downstairs drinking with Adam for half an hour until he thought it was safe to go upstairs.

When he did, he found Jessie in the bathroom with the door closed. Her weekend bag had been unpacked and was tucked away in a corner while the king-size bed loomed in the middle of the room.

He sipped his drink. He didn't know how he was going to sleep next to Jessie for the next three nights without kissing her, touching her, making love to her. The almost kiss a few months ago and that moment by the helicopter had cracked something open in him. On the one hand, he wanted to explore what they could have. On the other, he knew, like Adam said, he was playing with fire. Downstairs, Adam told him he and Tia had invited a few other singles to their dinner at a local restaurant. Perhaps he should keep his options open and not be too quick to leap into something with Jessie when she'd only given him some knowing glances and looks, but she hadn't exactly stuck her tongue down his mouth to show him she wanted him.

The bathroom door opened and Jessie emerged in

the itsy bittiest shorts he'd ever seen and a halter top revealing a smooth expanse of shoulder and a deep V that revealed the swell of her small but round breasts.

Ryan swallowed. "What are you wearing?"

Jessie smiled and Ryan felt his groin swell. "It's hot out and I wanted to get comfortable. Dinner isn't for another few hours." She came toward him, took the tumbler out of his hand, placed it to her generous mouth and took a sip.

"Strong." She handed it back to him. "I think I need something sweet and fruity."

What Ryan saw in front of him could certain qualify as both. And if he had his wish, he'd be indulging all weekend.

"Are you coming?"

Ryan blinked and realized Jessie was standing in the doorway. "No, you go ahead. I'll change, as well."

"All right. I'll see you downstairs."

Ryan breathed a sigh of relief when the door closed. He sat on the accent chair on the opposite side of the room and inhaled deeply. He had to calm himself, because if he didn't, he'd be hauling Jessie back into the bedroom.

Jessie was thankful for a few moments to herself while Ryan stayed in the guest room. When he'd been downstairs, she'd taken a moment to gather herself. She'd talked herself off the ledge about sharing a bedroom with Ryan. Like Tia said, they were two adults. Surely they could *platonically* share a bed together for a few days.

But then Ryan had come into the room and the way his eyes raked hers, Jessie was starting to believe she might be in trouble.

"Jessie, come on over." Adam caught sight of her in the foyer. "Have a drink."

Smiling, she walked over to join him and his wife at the bar and slid onto a bar stool. Tia was busy putting out chips and salsa on the countertop.

"What can I get you?" Adam inquired.

Jessie motioned to the pitcher of red liquid with fruit. "Is that sangria?"

"It's my specialty," Tia answered. "Would you like some?"

"Would love some," Jessie replied. "This place is great." She spun around and looked over the expansive living room with its wood-burning fireplace. She also liked that she could see the hexagon-shaped breakfast room and high-backed chairs that went with the wood table. The kitchen was spectacular, complete with stainless-steel appliances.

"Thank you," Adam said. "Here's your sangria." He handed her a glass and then raised his beer to tip against her glass. *"¡Salud!"*

"¡Salud!"

The doorbell rang and Adam went to answer it. Another couple came in, waving as Ryan rambled down the stairs. While Adam helped them with their bags, Ryan waved Jessie over to meet them.

"Jessie…" Ryan slid his arm around Jessie's shoulders. It was a casual but somewhat proprietary gesture. "I'd like you to meet my good friends, Mike and Corinne."

The couple complemented each other with their pale skin and dark hair. Corinne was tall and willowy with striking gray-blue eyes. Mike had a slim, athletic frame, a bald head and brown eyes. Husband and wife were both casually dressed in shorts and T-shirts for the weekend.

"Great to meet you both," Jessie said.

"I'll show you your room," Adam chimed in. "Follow me." He led them up the stairs.

"What are you drinking?" Ryan asked.

"Homemade sangria." Jessie licked her lips and found Ryan watching the movement. She quickly stepped out of his embrace, toward the kitchen where Tia had set out some fruit and cheese. Jessie reached for a cube of cheddar cheese, desperate to do something to escape the sexual tension in the air.

"Great spread," Ryan commented to Tia, who was busy arranging hummus and veggies on a platter.

"Why, thank you." Tia smiled. "I love to entertain, but this will tide you over until dinner. Adam made reservations at his favorite spot in town."

Eventually Adam, Mike and Corinne joined them downstairs, and they all drank and nibbled on the munchies Tia had laid out.

"It's great to finally meet the infamous Jessie," Mike commented as they stood around in the kitchen. "Ryan has talked about you often, but were beginning to think you were a figment of his imagination."

The entire group laughed, but Ryan didn't appear as

amused as the rest of his friends. "Oh, I'm very much real," Jessie replied. "But I admit I've been a bit busy trying to get my law career off the ground that I've taken this one—" she motioned to Ryan at her side "—for granted. But not anymore." She winked at him.

And she hoped he knew she meant it. Jessie had recognized that she'd turned her back on her oldest friend, who been there when she'd scraped her knee or fallen off her bike. Or when she'd cried when her parents had made her get braces, even though Ryan had soon been sporting a set, as well. He'd always been by her side and this weekend it was her turn.

"To friendship!" Adam held up his beer bottle and everyone raised their glasses.

Jessie glanced up to find Ryan's eyes on her and, once again, her insides clenched. She bit down on her lip and forced herself to remain calm. Surely she could handle a few hours in his company at dinner, in a public place surrounded by his friends? Resolution filled her. By the end of the evening, she would have tamped down on her desire for Ryan, otherwise they wouldn't be able to share a bed together.

The trendy seafood restaurant they went to later that evening was great and so was the company. Their group of eight consisted of two couples—Adam and Tia, Mike and Corinne—and four singles—Ryan, Jessie, Dean and Lauren. Dean and Lauren had arrived shortly before they'd left the house. They were both blond and blue-eyed—Jessie could see why Tia and Adam were trying to hook the two of them up.

The food was passed family-style across the table and the wine flowed freely. Over dinner, Jessie discovered they'd gone to Columbia with Ryan, which was how they all knew each other. Despite her going to NYU, they didn't make Jessie feel like the odd woman out. She couldn't remember a time when she was so relaxed and at ease, but she supposed she'd always felt that way in Ryan's presence. He had a natural way about him that was reassuring.

Corinne commented on how Jessie and Ryan suited each other. "You say you're just friends, but you guys finish each other's sentences and you know what food the other likes."

Ryan hadn't even bothered passing the peel-and-eat shrimp appetizer to Jessie because he knew Jessie didn't care for shrimp, though she'd killed her king crab entrée. And when Tia had given Ryan the sautéed Brussel sprouts with bacon, Jessie commented on how he hated the vegetable.

"They're like an old married couple," Mike said from Corinne's side.

"Was that supposed to be a put-down?" Ryan asked with a laugh, placing his arm along the back of Jessie's chair, which she seemingly didn't mind. "I think there's something to be said for knowing another person, better than they maybe even know themselves."

Jessie turned to look at Ryan, but she couldn't read his expression. She glanced around the table and the others were exchanging knowing glances. *Did they know something she didn't?* She felt exposed.

"So how did your job interview go with Black Crescent?" Dean suddenly inquired of Ryan.

Jessie rolled her eyes upward. She was thankful that Dean changed the topic—she'd wanted to be off the hot seat—but didn't like the new focus of conversation.

"I'm surprised you want to man that damaged ship," Mike said. "I mean didn't the original owner, Vernon Somebody, run off with everyone in town's money?"

"Yeah, Vernon Lowell pretty much bankrupted the entire town," Dean replied. "What gives? Why would you want any part of it?"

Ryan looked at Jessie. Was her face burning because she could feel herself becoming flushed? He had to know she hated to talk about this. "Because I can change everyone's perception."

"If anyone can, it's Ryan," Adam said from across the table.

Jessie sensed Adam was trying to help by boosting Ryan's ego, but she didn't care. Vernon Lowell's machinations had left her family penniless and they were discussing it over dessert as if it meant nothing. Unsure how much more she could take, Jessie fidgeted in her chair, eager to move on to another topic.

"Why is Joshua Lowell leaving anyway?" Mike asked. "Or is he exactly like his father and turning tail and running?"

"Rumor is he has a lovechild out there somewhere. They could be worth a lot of money since his father probably has it all secretly hidden somewhere," Dean stated.

Ryan must have sensed her unease, because he

said, "Does it matter? It's all conjecture, anyway, and shouldn't be believed."

Jessie had had enough. "If you'll excuse me." She pushed out her chair quickly and rushed out of the room. Instead of heading for the bathroom, she went to a side door. She heard footsteps behind her but kept going.

Once outside, she bent over and breathed in deeply. The door opened and she saw men's shoes. She didn't have to stand up to know Ryan had followed her.

"Are you okay?"

Jessie straightened and narrowed her gaze at him. "What do you think?"

He glanced beside him. "I'm sorry about that. None of my friends know about your family's past with Black Crescent. I've never broken your confidence and shared it with anyone."

"Not even Adam?"

"No."

Jessie had to admit she was impressed because, over the course of the evening, she'd seen how close the two men were. "Thank you, but I don't think even you get it."

"Get what?"

"How hard it is to one day to wake up and find all your money is gone along with all the dreams and hopes you had for yourself and your family. That's what my father felt. You have no idea what it's like to walk a day in my shoes, to endure the whispers and pitying glances from your classmates who know your family has literally been wiped out by the snap of a finger."

"Jessie…" Ryan made to come toward her, but Jessie held out her hand.

"Black Crescent changed the course of my life, my future, influencing the decisions I've made. And ever since that anniversary article came out, I've had to relive the most difficult time of my entire life. I thought I was behind it, but hearing your friends laughing and joking in there about how Vernon destroyed our town… Well, it didn't affect them. It affected me." She pounded her chest.

"I get it, sweetheart." This time, Ryan moved until he was a few inches away. She saw him hesitate for a second before putting his arm around her.

"Maybe a little." She leaned into him and accepted the comfort he was offering, "But haven't you wondered why I live in New York?" She pushed away slightly to look up at him and felt tears leaking from her lids. "Because I can be anonymous. Everyone in Falling Brook knows my sorry history, but in the city, I can be someone different. I've reinvented myself."

"Yes, you have," Ryan said, wiping the tears from her cheeks with the pad of his thumb. "But you have nothing to be ashamed of. What happened wasn't your fault. You were a child."

"I know that here—" Jessie pointed to her temple "—but not here." She patted her heart.

"You've accomplished so much, Jessie," Ryan stated. "Don't lose sight of that. Despite everything that happened to you, you finished college and law school. You're a lawyer for Christ's sake! I'm sorry to tell you, but not every one of our Falling Brook classmates fared as well."

Jessie thought back to their reunion. Ryan was right. Jessie had been surprised at the strides she'd made in the last ten years over her peers. "You're saying all this because you're my friend."

His expression was dark and serious. "No, I'm not. I'm saying it because you're *you*."

Before she could guess his next action, Ryan hooked an arm around her waist and pulled her tight against him.

Jessie looked up into his eyes and was lost. How could she have denied herself this magic when she wanted him? She pulled his head down so his mouth was just above hers. Then she pressed her lips against his and it unleashed a longing deep in her body. She grabbed his biceps as her overloaded senses took in that she was kissing Ryan. His mouth was smooth, questing with the right amount of pressure. Glorious, heady sensations took over Jessie, burning her skin from the inside out. Ryan devoured her mouth as if he was in the desert sand and she was his water.

When his tongue teased her lips apart and swept inside her mouth, her body took over and Jessie began kissing him back. She followed his lead as he delved deeper into the heat of her mouth. Their tongues slid along each other's in an erotic duel. Her nipples turned erect against the fabric of her dress and she restlessly moved against him, wanting more. Ryan pressed her tightly to him and she felt the swell of his manhood.

A loud cough from behind startled them, causing

Ryan to suddenly release her. Jessie, embarrassed to see a restaurant worker had stumbled across them, immediately rushed through the doors until she found the ladies' room.

"Jessie, wait!" Ryan called after her, but she didn't stop. She needed distance. *Now.*

Ryan's head fell back against the wall of the restaurant as his brain struggled to process what had just happened.

He'd kissed *Jessie*!

He'd always felt that, if given the chance, they could be good together. He hadn't been wrong. The heat they'd created had been nothing short of sensational. He hadn't been thinking when he'd closed the distance between them and taken her mouth in an insistent kiss that left no room for hesitation. She'd responded when he'd slid his tongue inside her mouth and met his tongue with her own. The way she'd moved against him would have made a strong man weak.

The feel, the taste of her on his mouth, was like forbidden fruit in the Garden of Eden and he'd sampled. The irrational part of his brain wanted to know how far they would have gone if they hadn't been interrupted. But they had been and Jessie had run like her pants were on fire.

Where did they go from here?

Five

Jessie stared at her reflection in the mirror of the restaurant's bathroom and what she saw there scared her. Her pupils were dilated, her cheeks were flushed and her breaths were coming in shallow gulps. What she saw was desire. Pure and strong. She'd thought she was immune and could control it. *Had her desire for Ryan always been there waiting to emerge if presented the opportunity?* How else to explain that they'd made out?

She closed her eyes and attempted to calm her nerves, but she couldn't. No matter how hard she tried, she couldn't forget Ryan's mouth on hers. The *taste* of him. The scent of his cologne and the warmth of his skin through his button-down shirt. It was all right there in vivid high definition in her mind.

She wouldn't be able to put him in a box and tuck

it away as she'd done with that almost kiss on reunion night. She'd done her best to act as if it had been an anomaly. A moment in time in which they'd both been carried away. But tonight was different. She'd willingly participated in the kiss and, if they hadn't been interrupted, she'd have asked for more because it was *that* good. The attraction she'd felt for Ryan blew her mind.

Jessie couldn't recall a time in which she'd felt that way when Hugh kissed her. She'd never experienced the all-consuming lust she'd felt in those few minutes she'd shared with Ryan in any of her encounters with Hugh. Hugh was the only man Jessie had ever been with. Although there been other opportunities in college and again in law school, Jessie had remained true to Hugh. Plus, the intimacy she'd shared with Hugh had always been pleasant enough, but there had never been fireworks like the kind she'd felt just now with Ryan.

She knew she had to go back to the table with Ryan and the other couples and feign that what had happened, hadn't. How was she supposed to act? *How would he?* She knew they needed to talk, but she wasn't sure what she would say. She would have to fake it until she made it.

Summoning all her courage, Jessie left the restroom.

Ryan was waiting for her in the corridor. His hungry eyes soaked in hers and her stomach wanted to melt in a puddle, but it didn't. "Are you okay?" he inquired.

She nodded. Her vocal cords were unable to speak. "About—"

She stopped him and put her fingertips to his mouth.

"Can we not analyze it right now and get back to the dinner?"

His eyes shuttered at her dismissal and she recognized that she'd hurt him. "If that's what you want."

"I do."

"Very well, then." He motioned for her to precede him. "After you."

When they returned to the table, everyone glanced up at them. *Were they all assuming she and Ryan had snuck away to make out?* Because they'd be right.

"We were wondering where you two had disappeared to," Adam said with a bemused smile. "We're going to head back to the house, if you're ready?"

"We are," Jessie and Ryan said simultaneously.

The group laughed because once again they were in unison, like everyone had teased earlier. And maybe they were, but on that terrace, their relationship shifted and there was no going back.

The ride in Adam's Escalade was uncomfortable to say the least. Ryan didn't attempt to make polite chit-chat. When he'd met Jessie in the restaurant corridor, he'd hoped they would talk. He'd known it was an inconvenient time, but he'd hoped that maybe she'd finally admit they should pursue whatever it was between them. But instead he'd been shot down. Jessie wanted to sweep the kiss underneath the rug and he was pissed off about it.

When they made it to the house, Jessie rushed off upstairs. Dean and Lauren went to their respective rooms while Mike and Corinne departed quickly. Ryan figured the married couples wanted to be alone, because Adam and Tia were right behind them, but he stopped Adam on the steps.

"I'll be right up, babe," Adam told Tia.

"I'll be waiting." She winked at her husband and left the two men alone.

Adam turned to Ryan. "What's up? As you can see—" he glanced up the stairs "—I have a hot date."

Ryan grinned. "I won't keep you. I just need some linens and a pillow. I'm going to sleep on the couch."

"Really? The vibe I got when you guys came back to the table led me to believe…"

Ryan rolled his eyes. "Nothing is going to happen. So, if you don't mind, I need those linens."

Adam stared at him for several beats. "All right, I'll be right back." He ran up the stairs and Ryan followed him. He would only be in his and Jessie's room long enough to get something to sleep in and return downstairs.

When he arrived, Jessie was in the bathroom, brushing her teeth. She had already changed into some sort of matching pajama set with a camisole and shorts. Had to be some sort of record for getting undressed. Guess she wanted to be sure she was nowhere around when he came in. *What did she think was going to happen? That he would jump her bones the minute they were alone?* He'd gotten the message: their first kiss had been a mistake.

Ryan walked to the doorway. "I'm going to sleep on the couch downstairs."

Jessie eyes grew wide and then she rinsed and wiped

her mouth with a towel from a nearby rack. "That's probably best."

He glared at her. So that's the way she wanted to play this? Had the kiss meant nothing to her? He most certainly was having trouble remembering why he'd insisted to himself and his friends any attraction he'd felt was over.

"All right. Well…good night. I'll see you in the morning." Ryan grabbed his toiletry bag and some shorts and a T-shirt from his suitcase, and left the room.

He ambled down the stairs and found a pillow and a blanket waiting for him on the sofa. He stared at the midsize sofa. It didn't look very comfortable and he was not excited to sleep on it, but what choice did he have?

After using the half bath to brush his teeth, Ryan came back to the living room and proceeded to prepare himself a makeshift bed on the sofa. He didn't bother changing. It was going to be a long night anyway. Lying down, he stared up at the ceiling, reliving the kiss with Jessie in his mind.

The kiss had warmed him. He'd felt the scorch of her lips on his and the taste of her on his tongue. Sleep would be a long time coming because he doubted he could rid his mind of the feeling of holding the woman he'd always wanted in his arms. Their first kiss was everything he'd dreamed of and more. Now his emotions felt pummeled because of Jessie's refusal to acknowledge they could be so much more.

Ryan sat upright. Maybe some ocean air would help him find peace and the sleep he needed. But first he was going for a glass of brandy. He found Adam's favorite sitting on the counter with the other alcohol. After pouring himself more than two thumbs in a tumbler, Ryan made his way through the French doors and out onto the wraparound terrace.

It was dark, but there were thousands of tiny stars in the sky and, with the full moon, it was enough for Ryan to see his drink. He leaned against the balustrade and sipped his brandy.

He didn't know how long he was out there, musing over the night's events, when the creek of the floorboards forced him to stand upright.

As if he'd conjured her up, Jessie was standing by the French doors. His eyes ate her up, loving the sight of her shapely legs in shorts that barely reached her lush thighs.

"Go to bed, Jessie." He turned away and stared back at the dark night sky. It was late and he wasn't in the mood to dissect the kiss, their relationship, or anything else. If she didn't go right now, he wasn't sure of his next actions.

"I can't. We need to talk."

The words every man dreaded.

Ryan turned to face her. "You first."

Jessie felt the anger emanating from Ryan and knew it was directed at her for not confronting the kiss earlier. She'd run because she'd been too afraid to face what had happened. She'd tried to put the mask on, layer by layer, but had failed miserably. Was it any surprise that when she'd tried to go to bed, she couldn't sleep? She'd tossed and turned until she'd finally given up the ghost and realized that until she settled things with Ryan, sleep would elude her.

Jessie had come downstairs to find him, but not before she'd shocked herself by taking the spare condom she kept in her purse and placed it in her pocket. Was she hoping for something more? Maybe. But when she'd seen the empty couch, her heart had lurched. She'd wondered if she'd pushed Ryan away enough to make him leave, but instead she'd found him on the deck looking out over the ocean, his button-down shirt nearly undone and still wearing his jeans.

"You're angry with me."

"Does that surprise you?"

She shook her head. "No. I suppose not. I deserve it for being a coward." The kiss had left her feeling vulnerable and exposed.

"Go on." He sipped the drink in his hand.

"The kiss caught me off-guard. We've always been friends, but everything has changed and…"

"That scares you," Ryan finished. "Do I scare you? Or is this because you're still with Hugh?"

"I—I'm not with Hugh anymore. We're on a break."

"A break?" Ryan asked, straightening. "Since when?"

Jessie walked over to him at the balustrade and glanced at the dark ocean.

"Jessie?"

She turned to him and his gaze focused on her. "Since the night of the reunion."

Ryan's eyes darkened and Jessie forced herself to swallow. "Why didn't you tell me?"

Jessie cocked her head to one side. "Do you really

have to ask me? Because *everyone*, especially my parents, think Hugh and I are supposed to be together. But they couldn't be more wrong."

"How long have you been feeling this way?"

Jessie shrugged. "A while. I've been restless and unsure of our relationship for some time… But I've felt so ruled by Black Crescent's fall and my parents' expectations to marry a guy like Hugh, from an established wealthy family, that I've pushed aside my own feelings. And when we nearly kissed at the reunion, it threw me for a loop. Just like tonight did. I couldn't continue seeing him if I had feelings for another man."

Ryan's gaze locked with hers and then he drew her to him. Pinning her against him, his mouth sought hers. Sky and earth tilted on its axis for Jessie as Ryan's lips parted hers in a kiss that was everything she'd ached for but hadn't realized she needed. And in that devastating moment, Jessie knew that she would die if she couldn't be with him. Is that why, in a spur-of-the-moment decision, she'd put a condom in her pocket?

When Ryan pulled away, he held both sides of her face and peered into her eyes. "Tell me to stop, Jessie, because I don't know if I can."

"I don't want you to stop, Ryan. I need you."

He leaned his forehead against hers, his lips a fraction away. "You're temptation for even the strongest man. You have no idea how much I want to make love to you."

She gasped and, that very instant, his mouth was back on hers. Jessie didn't have any doubts. She wanted Ryan. She didn't know if she always had. She did know that in this moment she had to have him. His fingers tangled in her hair and brought her forward to his mouth. Oh how she wanted that mouth. That beautiful mouth.

They kissed and kissed and then kissed again. He pulled away a few times to move from her lips to kiss his way down her throat to her neck, but then he'd return to her mouth as if he couldn't keep away.

Sensation engulfed her as she concentrated wholly on Ryan and vice versa. It was crazy to think she was on fire for her friend, but she was. The emotions she felt were real. Jessie melted from the onslaught and didn't realize he was walking them somewhere. With his hands framing her face and without breaking the kiss, he'd moved Jessie up against the wall of the house. Their mouths opened so their tongues could taste each other deeply. His hand slid up and down her body until Jessie found her pajama camisole being lifted over her head and tossed aside.

He jerked his head back to look at her and Jessie basked in his openly hungry gaze. He wanted her and she wanted his mouth roving over every inch of her. What had started from a simple kiss on the dance floor three months ago had turned into hot, heavy need. Jessie ached and the only one who could soothe her was Ryan—and only if he was buried deep inside her.

She wanted to shout in delight when his hands finally encircled her breasts. Raw need ricocheted through her. With a feathered touch, Ryan skimmed the undersides and swell of her breasts before treating them to the touch of his lips and fingertips. They turned to peaks with his sensuous suckling and the cries echoing through the night weren't someone else's, but her own. Never had her breasts received such attention with a deliberate attempt to bring her pleasure. And he did. Ryan treated the other breast with equal attention and Jessie was lost, but not for long.

It was her turn to seize the moment. When he lifted his head, she quickly set about unbuttoning the last few buttons of his shirt. She heard Ryan catch his breath as she slid the shirt down his shoulders and biceps until it fell with a soft swoosh to the deck.

Jessie's greedy eyes looked their feel of his torso. Ryan had an amazing body, broad at the shoulders and slim at the hips, with defined, long muscles. They weren't overly developed or bulging, but would be enough for her to hold on to. He had an amazing ab eight-pack with a sprinkling of hair that arrowed below his washboard stomach to his jeans. Jessie couldn't help licking her lips. She wanted him in every way possible. She couldn't wait to feel him and to experience everything he could give her—release and completion.

She reached out and touched him. He was all heat and muscle, and she trembled with excitement at the feel of his skin on her hands. She ran her fingers through the hair on his chest and then lower to smooth down his abs. When she reached the waistband of his jeans, she fiddled with the snap until she could push his zipper and jeans down in one fell swoop, allowing his erection to spring free.

He stepped out of his jeans and her hand grasped his straining length. She stroked him gently. His nostrils flared and he choked a growl when she cupped and stroked him with both hands. "You're killing me, Jessie."

She wanted to do more, but her body was wet and damp and readying itself for his possession. She released him and, placing a hand on the back of his head, pulled him in for another dizzying kiss.

"I need you now," she murmured into his lips.

Ryan was spinning out of control. This was all moving too fast. Hell, he couldn't remember if he even had protection in his wallet. *Did he have one?* Think. But his brain was mush because kissing Jessie—the woman he'd adored from afar for nearly two decades—was making rational thought impossible.

He should regroup, slow the pace, but he didn't. Instead, reaching for her shorts, he quickly snatched them down her hips and dropped them to the floor. He was stunned to realize Jessie wasn't wearing any underwear. He had complete and unfettered access to her. For a second, his mind blanked. Luckily, Ryan knew his way around a woman's body and how to pleasure them. Satisfy them. Ryan was determined Jessie would be when he was done with her.

He dropped to his knees and, reaching for her curvy bottom, pulled her to his mouth. He teased the cleft of her sex with his tongue. He lifted his head and his eyes glowed when they connected with hers. "You're wet for me."

She nodded. "And you are hard for me."

Ryan grinned and then he made her even wetter.

He used his fingers to tease, swirl and stroke her sensitive numb. He knew Jessie wanted more, but instead he worked her with his fingers, going faster and faster. She opened her legs, stretching for him and riding his hand until he replaced those fingers with his mouth.

Jessie cried out at the lick of his tongue on her clitoris. So he continued kissing, licking and flicking her with his tongue. When she bucked, he added his digits again and sucked so deep on her nub that she came almost immediately. He rode the wave with her, his breath coming in unsteady gasps because he'd been right there with her. The speed they were going left him no doubt on the direction they were heading, but he wasn't sure about protection.

He rose off his haunches to fasten his mouth on hers for a quick searing kiss and then lifted his head. "I don't have a condom."

"Check…my…shorts," Jessie said on an uneven breath.

"What?" He was stunned, but leaned down to grab up her pajama bottoms that he'd tossed aside and indeed found a single condom packet in the pocket.

"Jessie Acosta! Did you come down here with the sole intention of seducing me?"

She blushed and looked away.

"Don't do that," Ryan said, clasping her chin in his hand and forcing her to look at him. "You wanted me. Don't be afraid to admit that."

She nodded. "I do, so don't make me wait another minute. Or do you need my help putting that thing on?"

He smirked. "No, I think I got this." Within seconds,

he'd sheathed himself, placed her hands on his shoulders and lifted her off the floor.

"Hook your legs around my hips." He knew he was being demanding, but Ryan was at the edge of control.

When she complied and wrapped herself around him, clinging to his shoulders, he brought them together in one slow, deliberate thrust.

Jessie's eyes snared his and she didn't look away, not even as he went deeper with the second thrust all while his hands were under her bottom, supporting her. Instead, she moved to meet him and a shudder went straight through Ryan. "Yes, babe. Just like that," he said through gritted teeth as he righted his balance so he could bear his weight and hers.

God, she felt so good. So wet. So right for him.

She wiggled and slid until she'd taken him to hilt. *Sweet Jesus!* This was going to be over before it began. Sucking in air, he fought to hold back and kissed her again, but Jessie was in control now. She was riding him and his grip grew stronger, his kisses became more frantic, trailing her face and down her neck as she rocked against him. Her breath was coming short and fast—faster and faster until she was panting.

If this was the road to heaven, Ryan didn't mind being on it.

Jessie was having an out-of-body experience. Her legs were curled tightly around Ryan's hips in a viselike grip. She'd never felt so completely and utterly abandoned during sex before. With Ryan, she could revel in her desire for him and he allowed her to do so without claiming victory for himself.

She whimpered in delight when he pushed inside, further and further, until her entire body absorbed him and the tension snapped. Waves of pleasure radiated through her, threatening to swallow her whole. Yet still she wanted *more, more, more.*

She coiled tighter around him and Ryan growled as he pumped up to meet her, supporting them both. When her screams threatened to wake the entire house, he grasped her by her hair and pulled her mouth to his in a hard and hungry kiss. Jessie gave as good as she got, because she craved this man with every cell of her body. Her lips weaved around his and her tongue sought entry into his mouth, fusing them closer and closer together.

She took all she could while demanding more. She devoured him and in return she found the purest pleasure she'd ever had her entire life. The flames inside her erupted when Ryan reached between them to press his thumb on that sensitive nub between her legs. She gave up the fight when her third orgasm surged through her, tightening her muscles around him as a bright light exploded behind her eyes. She clutched Ryan's shoulders and heard his growl of satisfaction as he, too, reached the peak of the mountain and came tumbling back down to earth.

Six

Ryan awoke the next morning in the guest room he and Jessie were sharing. They were sprawled across the bed with the covers and pillows strewed across it. Ryan's entire body was effused with satiation. He slid his hand through the spill of Jessie's hair lying like a silken cloud on his chest. She was draped over him after he'd devoted the morning hours to exploring her delectable body. He'd been fascinated by her reactions and her unabashed responsiveness. Jessie wasn't afraid to show how much she enjoyed making love with him. In fact, she'd been as eager as he was.

He'd been shocked when she'd told him of the condom in her pocket. That meant she'd come looking for him last night with the express intent of taking their relationship to the next level. She'd wanted *this*. *Him*.

Being with Jessie had been urgent and explosive. Thinking about the way her breasts had jounced up and down against him as she rode him was a turn-on. She'd welcomed him, wrapping her tight little body around him until he'd detonated like a rocket. He was afraid he'd become addicted because the more they did, the more he wanted. He wanted to obliterate any memory of Hugh in her mind and he was sure he had. They'd made love so many times, they'd finished a second pack of condoms.

Was it because making love with Jessie had been the culmination of years of wanting? Being with her was the most satisfying sexual experience of his life, more than any other lover he'd ever been with. It felt different. *Had he always known that?* Is that why he'd run as soon as Hugh came back into the picture? Or why he'd purposely set his sights on the Black Crescent job to alienate Jessie and ensure they'd never have a chance?

Jessie shifted to roll away but Ryan stopped her. "You're awake."

She nodded shyly.

"You okay?" He didn't know if he was asking for himself or for her. All he knew was that the closeness and intimacy they'd shared in the wee hours of the night and into this morning was real. Yet he didn't want to get ahead of himself and think it was more profound than it was. Yet he couldn't deny that, spectacular sex aside, Jessie meant something to him and always would.

"Yes."

"Any regrets?"

Jessie slid up his chest and, to his surprise and delight, swept her lips over his. Ryan didn't realize he'd been holding his breath waiting for the answer. When she lifted her head, her palm caressed his cheek.

"Ryan, last night was amazing. Incredible. Wonderful. I don't know how many more adjectives you need for me to describe it. I mean…" She glanced down and played with several hairs on his chest. "I never knew it could be that exciting, fun, *explosive*." She grinned.

"Neither did I, but I guess it's based on chemistry."

"Which we seem to have in spades." Jessie glanced at the clock. It read 10:00 a.m. "You realize we've been in bed for hours. What must your friends think?"

"They'll think we're grown adults who hooked up."

"Is that all we are?" Jessie asked expectantly.

"That depends. What do you want, Jessie?" Ryan asked. "I don't want to be your backup plan because things between you and Hugh have fallen apart and you need a soft landing."

Jessie sat upright, taking the duvet cover with her to cover her small breasts. "That's not what this is."

"I'm free, single and unencumbered," Ryan said.

"So am I."

He eyed her suspiciously.

"I admit, I may not be ready to jump into something serious. I enjoyed last night with you, Ryan, and I don't regret it. But we have crossed the line from friendship into something more."

"And?"

"I'm okay with seeing where this goes if you are."

He grinned. "I'm game."

"Good—" she threw off the duvet cover "—because I'd like to experience more of it."

Ryan raised a brow. "Oh, would you?"

She grinned mischievously. "Oh, absolutely."

Jessie stared at Ryan from behind her Guess sunglasses. He was playing football with Adam, Mike and Dean in the sand while the ladies—Jessie, Tia, Corinne and Lauren—were on their way to a great tan. He was bare-chested and wearing a pair of knee-length board shorts and all Jessie could think about was how soon they could go back to the bedroom.

It had damn near taken an act of God to get them out of there to begin with. They hadn't made it downstairs until nearly noon because they'd shared a long, hot shower wherein they'd both given and received pleasure. Jessie was on a natural high because sex with Ryan made her feel powerful, beautiful and bolder than she'd ever been in her life.

How was it that her supervixen urges were sky-high with Ryan, but nonexistent with Hugh? Hugh had commented on her lack of sex drive whenever they were intimate. Perhaps their lack of intimacy stemmed from Hugh symbolizing stability and her parents' wishes, not being her own, thus making their love life lackluster. Or was being with Ryan a rebellion against her parents and their expectations? Jessie wasn't sure if what was happening was for real.

"Must have had a great night," Tia commented from Jessie's side.

"Pardon?"

Tia looked at her incredulously. "C'mon, girl, we all know the two of you were getting busy all night and into the morning."

Jessie blushed several shades.

"The walls aren't soundproof," Tia commented, pointing toward the house.

Jessie was mortified that everyone in the house knew what they'd been up to, but Tia patted her thigh. "Girlfriend, don't be embarrassed. We were not paying you guys any mind because we were having fun of our own. I'm just saying that we are all adults here and you two are welcome to do what single adults who are attracted to each other do."

Jessie sighed. "I suppose."

"You like him, right?"

"If you heard us, then the answer is pretty obvious."

"Well then, enjoy him and forget about the rest. What's wrong with having a holiday fling?"

"Because it's Ryan," Jessie whispered. "He's my oldest friend. He knows everything about me."

"Including what turns you on." Tia winked.

"Tia!"

"Hey, don't be mad. I speak the truth. Sometimes it takes being with someone who knows you so completely, inside and out, that makes it so incredible."

Jessie nodded. "How are we going to navigate this outside in the real world? Because right now it feels as if we're a bubble and this is a moment outside of normal reality."

"Stop worrying about tomorrow and enjoy today,"

Tia said. "Or at least the next couple of days. Tomorrow's worries will be here soon enough."

Jessie supposed she was right. They could have this moment in time without her worrying about her parents' expectations, doing what was right or how their friendship might be impacted. But it was hard for her to do. She usually looked before she leaped, but last night she hadn't. Instead, she'd gone on instinct. The kiss at the restaurant had shocked her, leading her to believe Ryan was as attracted to her as she was to him. She'd take a gamble when she'd put the condom in her pocket, never imagining that they might really use it.

But they had.

She blushed, thinking about sex up against the wall with Ryan and how deep he'd buried himself inside her. It was amazing to think that, after all this time, it was Ryan who did it for her. Who made her feel sexy and desired.

As if he intuitively knew she was thinking of him, Ryan smiled in her direction and her stomach fluttered. Ryan gave her butterflies! Why had she never realized how great they could be together? Because she'd been so focused on Hugh, on her parents' choice, that she had underestimated Ryan. Hadn't given him a second look. But now she was giving him a first, second and third. And she couldn't wait for the evening to come so they could resume their activities.

"Someone is feeling himself," Adam said when they paused from playing tag football long enough to drink some Gatorade and wipe the sweat from their foreheads.

"What do you mean?" Ryan said, swigging the sports drink.

Adam laughed. "C'mon, bro. We all know you and Jessie got horizontal last night."

Ryan glared at him.

"Don't even try to deny it," Adam said in response to his look. "Tia and I found your makeshift bed unslept in this morning. And to make matters worse, you and Jessie didn't emerge from the guest bedroom until damn near noon."

Ryan sighed heavily. Adam was right. There was no denying his relationship with Jessie had turned intimate. "Okay, okay." Ryan admitted reluctantly, "Things between Jessie and I have taken an unexpected but pleasant turn."

"It's what you wanted, right?" Adam asked, glancing in the women's direction. "For Jessie to see you as someone other than a friend."

"Yes," he said, nodding. "I do. But you know sex always tends to bring complications."

"Exactly. You were hung up on this girl then you said you were done. Obviously, you're not over her, Ryan. Watch yourself. She'll be nothing but heartbreak."

Ryan understood what Adam was saying, but this was a temporary relationship and he was embracing the now and forgetting about tomorrow. What happens in the Hamptons stays in the Hamptons. They'd just fallen headlong into bed. He smiled. Well, the bed came later.

"What's so funny?" Adam asked.

"Nothing," Ryan said. "Let's head back to our women." He was going to take full advantage of every moment he had with Jessie this weekend. He wasn't going to waste a single minute.

Later that afternoon, while everyone else went back to the house, Jessie and Ryan stayed out on the beach, choosing to take a walk instead. She enjoyed being in the outdoors with the clear sky and blue water. Often she was indoors, whether in class, the library or at the law firm, that she had precious little time outdoors. Unconsciously, Jessie's hand slipped into Ryan's as they trudged through the sand.

Eventually they came to a sand dune and, after a short climb, Jessie realized there wasn't another soul on the small curve of private beach. No boats were in the distance, either.

"This is crazy, you know? You and me," Jessie said, swinging their arms.

"Is it?" Ryan asked.

"I never anticipated having these feelings for you," Jessie admitted. "I've always had a plan. Knew exactly where my life was going."

"And with whom?"

She stopped walking and turned to face Ryan. "I don't deny that I thought I was supposed to be in love by now. Me and Hugh. That was always the plan. Get married. Buy a house. Have two kids. Along the way, the pressure got to me and I got restless for something more. The anniversary article on Black Crescent didn't help and only reminded me of the fact."

"Am I a way for you to get out from under your parents' expectations and end your relationship with

Hugh?" His eyes were earnest yet cautious as they searched hers.

"My parents, my friends…everyone keeps telling me what a great catch Hugh is and I believed the hype. I was so faithful, I wasn't even tempted in college to stray from the preordained path set for me. Even after I graduated, I didn't look at anyone else until the night of the reunion. That's when I really *saw* you."

"And I saw you."

"The desire in your eyes scared me," Jessie said. "It was so open, so honest. I knew then I couldn't stay committed to Hugh. Otherwise, I'd be tempted to cheat, and that's just not me. I want to just enjoy each other without any pressure."

"Without any commitments?" Ryan added.

She nodded. "Can you accept that while we navigate this?"

"I can. As we discussed, this is temporary."

"I don't want to lose our friendship, Ryan. That scares me most of all."

He reached for her, enveloping Jessie in his arms. "You won't lose me as a friend." He stroked her hair and looked deep into her eyes. "I'll always be here for you."

She smiled. "Now that we have that settled, why don't you be here for me another way…" She circled her arms around his neck and brought his mouth down to hers. At first his lips merely grazed hers—rubbing lightly back and forth until she parted her mouth and reached up on tiptoe to demand more pressure.

Ryan gave it to her. His hand shifted her head firmly in place so his tongue could delve into her hungry mouth. He stroked her with purpose that left no doubt as to the explicitness of what he wanted. It was the same for Jessie. It was like Ryan had pushed her On button and she'd come to life. Jessie hadn't known her body was capable of humming with so much pent-up desire.

She pushed her body hard against his, reveling in the impact of his muscular chest against her. He slid his arms tighter and, with one hand low on her bottom, pulled her even closer. He rocked them both, mimicking the actions of sex and bringing her to a flashpoint.

"Ryan," she moaned and, before she knew it, they were sinking into the sand on their knees and falling backward, Jessie on top of him. They kissed greedily and possessively. His hands splayed across her back and her fingers dug into the nape of his neck until there wasn't a single part of their bodies not touching.

Jessie felt Ryan's arousal against her belly and everything inside her burned. When she stole a glance at him, his eyes pierced right into her soul and she knew it was the same for him, too. She felt his hand move underneath her cover-up, reaching for her bikini bottom and pressing his palm against her damp heat. She gasped into his mouth and reached for the band of his swim shorts. Caressing him, she kissed him hard.

Ryan grabbed her hand to steady her. "We don't have a condom," he said,

In that moment, Jessie wanted to say she didn't care because she was on the pill, but she'd always practiced safe sex and wasn't about to stop now.

"I'll still make it good for you," Ryan whispered.

His hand went beneath her bikini bottom and touched her intimately.

Shamelessly, Jessie rocked against him and Ryan delivered his promise to make it good by kneading and massaging her breasts and catching his mouth with hers. She loved the way he took over. And when he pushed a finger inside her, thrusting in and out, she began to squirm. She was so hot and wet, she groaned, raking her fingers down his back.

"Easy, love." Ryan flipped them over until he was leaning over her and Jessie was in the sand. Somehow it didn't matter because he was pushing her bikini aside so his tongue could feast on her nipples. She gripped his shoulders for support as a rush of heat surged through her.

"Oh my God…" She moaned as every cell of her body came alive.

Ryan continued paying homage to her breasts while his fingers gently yet ever so slowly found the swollen spot where she ached. With each stroke, Jessie became a live wire and when his thumb massaged her nub, Jessie couldn't hold back any longer. She shuddered, crying out as wave after wave of pleasure overtook her. As she floated back to reality, Jessie realized she felt languid and at ease.

"Feel better now?" Ryan asked softly in her ear.

It was the understatement of the year and she looked up at him, truly looked at him, and when she did, she noticed a sheen of sweat on his forehead. He was tightly coiled, all because he'd ensured she was satisfied first with no thought of his own needs.

"I do. But you—" She reached for his waistband, but he shook his head.

"Don't feel like you have to."

"But…"

"I wanted to give you pleasure. And you can return the favor tonight." He glanced at his watch. "We should go back, anyway. There's going to be a seafood boil tonight. And we don't want to be late again. Otherwise my friends will think we're sex addicts."

"If you're sure." She eyed him suspiciously. Hugh had always been about getting off first. Regardless of her satisfaction in the process.

He grinned. "I am." He rose and reached for her hand, pulling her to her feet as she adjusted her clothing.

"Where have you been all my life?" Jessie inquired.

"Next door."

Seven

Ryan stood on the porch holding a beer and watching Jessie as she cleaned up the dinner dishes. Adam and Tia had gone all out with good old-fashioned seafood boil complete with a beer base. It had been delicious and Ryan had the full belly to prove it. He couldn't remember when he'd had so much fun. He'd hung with his friends before in the Hamptons—Adam invited him all the time—but it was the first time he'd asked Jessie to join him. He thought he'd prove he'd conquered his attraction to Jessie, but he'd been wrong. Somehow this little trip had become more than he'd imagined. Yet it didn't change the facts. He wanted to run Black Crescent and Jessie…well, she was still as unsure of what she wanted as she'd ever been.

They'd gone from being next-door neighbors to

friends to lovers in the span of less than forty-eight hours and he'd loved every minute. Yet he knew eventually their time together would come to an end. It had to. He might have a bright future ahead with Black Crescent and Jessie needed to do some soul-searching.

That's not to say that being with Jessie wasn't spectacular. She'd blossomed in front of him and his friends. She held her own with the likes of Mike and Dean, easily bantering and trading teasing barbs with that brilliant smile of hers. She'd come alive in front of him and the sweet girl next door had been replaced with a sexy siren who burned hotter than any other woman he'd ever known. She was proud and confident. How else to explain how she'd literally brought him to his knees in the sand and unleashed his hedonistic affinities where anyone could have seen him giving her pleasure?

He'd worked until she'd screamed into blissful satiation. He'd known she hadn't been happy leaving him unsatisfied, but in that moment he hadn't minded abstaining. In fact, he could hardly think at the time because the attraction between them was so intense. In the past, he would have pushed for more, but he wasn't going to do that now because Jessie needed to make some choices about what she wanted in life.

"If I didn't know any better, I'd think you lovebirds were on your honeymoon," Adam said as he joined him on the porch.

Ryan looked at him in surprise.

"I saw the look you sent Jessie from across the room. It was like you have eyes for her and her alone."

"Suppose that's true," Ryan said. The sexual tension between them was too fraught to ignore. He supposed it was because hidden, long-denied feelings had bubbled to the surface and he was indulging over and over and over again.

"Uh-oh, she's headed this way and looking at you like you're the tasty morsel she can't wait to have. If you'll excuse me, I'm going to find my woman," Adam said with a laugh.

Jessie joined Ryan, her gaze colliding with his as electricity arced between them. "Hey, you."

"Don't look at me like that." Ryan swigged his beer.

"Like what?"

Ryan raised an eyebrow. "You know how. If you don't stop, I'm going to take you upstairs and have my way with you."

"Would that be so wrong?" she asked, moving closer and wrapping her arms around his midsection.

"It is if the evening is barely over," Ryan whispered. "The group was talking about going to a club tonight."

"Sounds like fun. I haven't been dancing in ages."

"You want to go?"

She nodded. "Usually, I'm pouring over briefs and doing research until my eyes droop closed. This weekend is my time to relax and let loose."

Ryan wondered if that's all he was to her. Freedom from the strict regime she'd placed herself under. "Then let's do that."

Thirty minutes later, after changing into club gear, Ryan heel-tapped the floor, waiting for Jessie to come downstairs. She'd asked him to wait for her so she could make an appearance. When she did, his eyes traveled

over every inch of her. The short skirt was nearly inde-
cent because it reached her mid-thigh and the sparkly
halter top wasn't much better. It was backless, which
meant she wasn't wearing a bra underneath. Ryan was
going to have a hard time focusing with Jessie looking like that.

"You like?" she asked, twirling in her four-inch heels.

"Yeah." He came toward her and traced the long
stretch of exposed bare thigh. "But I would prefer it if
you had on more clothes."

"Oh, don't be a spoilsport." She sidled next to him.
"I promise I'll make it worth your while later."

"You promise?" he whispered.

"Absolutely." She winked. "You're guaranteed to get
lucky."

Having Jessie on his arm made Ryan feel like the
luckiest guy in the world. He was both jealous and proud
of the envious looks they received when they made it to
the popular Hamptons' club. Adam had ensured they
were seated in VIP, but Jessie didn't care. She was itch-
ing to get on the dance floor.

"You don't dance?"

Ryan shrugged. He didn't usually, but for her, he
could be compelled to make an exception.

"Don't tell me you have no rhythm?" she teased.

"I can hold my own, but I wouldn't mind watching you."

She grinned mischievously. "C'mon, girls." She
grabbed Tia, Corinne and Lauren and corralled them
onto the dance floor.

Ryan watched in amusement as she positively strutted onto the floor with the ladies and got her groove on. The music was loud and he loved watching Jessie move and gyrate. She was all fluid grace. There was a freedom to her as she swished and sashayed her hips. Ryan could feel himself getting turned on. Apparently he wasn't the only one because another guy came over and began dancing with Jessie.

Ryan's fists curled. He wanted to punch the guy in the face, but instead he unclenched them and walked straight toward her.

"Excuse me," Ryan said, cutting into their dance, uncaring of the other man and pulling Jessie into his arms. "The lady is with me."

Jessie had never seen this side of Ryan. His aura commanded respect. He was broader in the shoulders than the man she'd been dancing with and the other man had easily capitulated and stepped back. Despite herself, Jessie loved Ryan going totally caveman and capturing her in his hold. Her body instinctively turned to him, but his look was dangerous. His hand grasped a handful of hair and tilted her face up to his.

"For the duration of the night, you're dancing with me, got it?"

She glanced up at him and was mesmerized by the slightly dangerous look in his eyes. She nodded. His hand slid around her and pulled her that bit tighter to him. Now she was wholly pressed up against him, chest-to-chest and thigh-to-thigh.

Ryan didn't say anything else. He didn't need to because the close proximity of their bodies said it all.

All she could do was move with him in a slow and easy rhythm. Just like he did in bed, Ryan guided her where he wanted her to go. When he inserted a jeans-clad thigh between hers, need slammed into Jessie. She was uncomfortably warm even though she was wearing very little.

That's what Ryan did to her. He made her hot and bothered, and she was powerless to fight it. Not when he used the setting and crowded dance floor to crush her to him. If he continued this dirty dancing routine, she'd been hiking up her skirt and begging him to take her on the dance floor.

Like you did at the beach?

Jessie blushed when she thought about how abandoned she'd been. If it hadn't been for Ryan thinking about protection and being safe, she would have allowed him to have her right there in the sand where anyone could have come across them.

"Tonight you're mine," Ryan whispered.

And he was right.

She had the damp thong to prove it.

Later, after they'd gotten hot and sweaty bumping and grinding at the club, they returned to the beach house. Mindless of the other couples, they'd gone straight to the room. Jessie was desperate for a shower, but also for Ryan to take her to paradise.

He must have been as frantic as she was because they both stripped on their way to the bathroom. She turned on the shower and stood under the steaming water, allowing the spray to pummel away her tension. At the sound of the shower door creaking, Jessie turned around in enough time to see Ryan sporting a massive erection.

"I'm calling in my marker," Ryan said with a wide grin as he came closer, joining her in the shower. "I'm ready to get lucky." He kissed her, deep and erotic, with slow yet firm kisses. His lips nipped and his tongue slid—it was an art form Ryan had mastered quite well.

As the water sluiced over his brown skin, Jessie slid her palms across his chest. She loved that he'd kept the lights off. Now Jessie could explore him by touch and not by sight. Blind to everything but him, she lowered her head to brush soft kisses against his wet skin. When she came to the dark disks of his nipples, her lips circled them, licking and flicking with her tongue. Ryan shuddered. That didn't stop her, Jessie sank to her knees and reached for his length. *She* was making the choice to please him because it felt right in the moment and because it was what she wanted.

She gripped the base of his erection and he groaned. She licked the head of him and Ryan's entire body tensed. So she did it again, swirling her tongue over the thick ridge. She opened her mouth and took him fully in. She pleasured him, pumping her hand to match the movement of her mouth. She loved the taste of him, the scent of him, and as his breathing became more labored, it turned her on.

"Jessie…" he gasped. "You have to stop…"

She lifted her head and looked up at him. "I'm not stopping." She wanted him to come as hard and loud as she had on the sand dune. His eyes were closed and she sensed he was fighting her, holding back, so she firmed her grip and increased her speed and suction. It didn't take long for Ryan to groan loudly as he came in her mouth.

Jessie, impressed she could bring this strong, exciting man joy, licked her lips. She rose and quickly found her back pressed against the cool wet tiles as Ryan returned the favor by licking down her torso.

"You enjoyed tormenting me—didn't you?—even though I was doing my best to keep you at bay," he inquired. His hands cupping her breasts, he lifted them to his mouth and began tonguing them generously.

"I did," she panted. The cloak of velvety darkness made it easy to soak up his watery caresses.

"I'm going to give it right back." He used his fingers and mouth to bring Jessie to peak, causing her orgasm to knife through her. Jessie lost her mind and screamed, but Ryan continued lapping her with his tongue through the spasms.

When the water became too cold from all their ministrations, they abandoned the shower. Not bothering with towels, they landed on the bed in a hot, damp tangle of limbs. Their mouths and hands spoke, kissing and touching and roving each other from head to toe until eventually Jessie couldn't take any more foreplay. With a firm grip, she grasped his length and guided him home.

He gasped, but didn't stop her. Instead, he let her climb on top and ride him hard. She kept it crazy fast until they were both teetering on the edge. She waited for him, eager to climax together, and they did in one harsh breath.

Eight

The Fourth of July came in with a bang. *Literally for Ryan.* Last night with Jessie was nothing short of incredible. Usually he didn't care for women to please him that way, but Jessie? She was another story altogether. He enjoyed the way she'd used her mouth, tongue and hands to take him over the edge. And yet he'd still found the energy to make love to her after.

Now they were on the deck of Adam's father's yacht, enjoying the sun and great weather before returning later to attend a party. It was impossible not to notice Jessie in the sarong she wore over the gold bikini.

Ryan refused to let feelings that were trying to emerge for Jessie free. They'd made a pact that this holiday weekend was temporary and purely fun. He had to remember that and not let Jessie get under his skin. Had she always been there, just beneath the surface and he'd clamped it down?

At the stern of the yacht, he saw Mike taking one of two Jet Skis out and followed him. "Can I take one for a ride?" he asked the yacht crew member.

"Sure."

He was climbing on when Jessie came rushing toward him. "Can I come?"

He had hoped to use the fresh air and speed to help clear his mind of the woman who'd seemed to invade all his senses for the last couple of days, but he couldn't very well turn her down. "C'mon, hop on."

Jessie quickly tossed aside her sarong and stepped down to the docking platform to climb onto the Jet Ski. Feeling her snugly settled behind him, her arms held tightly around his waist, was the last thing Ryan needed. "Hold on."

He started the engine and opened the throttle, sending the Jet Ski skimming over the ocean. It was exhilarating feeling the wind whip around his face, and exactly what he'd needed. Jessie was enjoying it, as well, because she tapped his shoulders to point out several things of interest.

When they returned to the yacht, Ryan felt in control of himself. He had to be. Tomorrow they would be returning to the real world where Jessie wasn't wholly his anymore and he couldn't spend every waking minute with her. They would both go back to work, to their own lives. He would return to his quest to be CEO of Black Crescent and turn the small-town hedge fund into a household name. Maybe then he'd feel satisfied with his life and good enough that a woman like Jessie would want to be on his arm.

Would she go back to Hugh?

His anger deepened because Ryan wanted a relationship with Jessie other than sex. Sure, they were sexually compatible in ways he'd never been with another woman, but he wanted *more*.

She'd indicated a restlessness with her life and her family expectations and being obligated to marry Hugh. But would she really change? Or was being with him just a rebellion against her family? Ryan didn't know for certain, but one thing he was sure of was that he wouldn't settle for being second best. Once the weekend was over, he would dismiss her from his life again and focus on his future at Black Crescent.

"What's wrong?" Jessie frowned as they turned the Jet Ski over to a crew member.

"Nothing."

She carefully studied him as she put her sarong back on. "Are you sure? You looked angry about something. Didn't you enjoy the ride?"

Oh yes, Ryan had enjoyed the ride the last few days; he was afraid of what would happen when the weekend was over.

Jessie couldn't put her finger on it, but something was definitely bothering Ryan. Since their return from Jet Skiing, he'd been more reserved, even standoffish. The last couple of days, he'd always been by her side with his arm casually wrapped around her. And she hated to admit it, but she kind of liked it. Hugh hated to show public displays of affection. So she'd gotten used to keeping her emotions in check. But with Ryan, he was so warm, so open, she rather liked the way he kissed her in front of his friends. He was unapologetic about his interest in her and she dug that about him.

She would get to the bottom of whatever was troubling him. Although tomorrow loomed, signaling the end of their three-day fling, she didn't want anything to spoil the perfect weekend they'd shared.

She reached inside the bucket of beer by the bar, pulled one out for him and one for herself, and joined him as he looked out over the water. "Everything okay?" she asked, handing him a beer.

"Thanks." He tipped his beer to hers. "I'm fine. Why do you ask?"

She shrugged. "I don't know. You seem *off* today."

"I was thinking about tomorrow when this all comes to an end."

She stared up into his brown eyes. "Don't do that. Don't let reality seep in yet. We're supposed to enjoy our time here without a care or worry. Remember?"

"It's not that easy."

"Yes. It is. We'll deal with tomorrow when it comes. Now, c'mon." She pulled him over to where the rest of his friends were gathered in the hot tub. Jessie threw off her sarong. She knew the tiny gold triangles of material that made up the top of her gold bikini barely covered her breasts.

Jessie had to admit she like how his eyes gleamed when his gaze dropped to the swell of her breasts. Heat surged through her and her nipples puckered. She was glad to be sinking into the hot, bubbling water because then Ryan wouldn't know the potent effect he had on her. Hugh was dead wrong. She didn't have a low sex drive. It just took the right man to bring it out of her.

She watched Ryan whip his T-shirt off and set it beside her sarong before joining her in the hot tub. Her eyes were hidden behind her oversize sunglasses so no one could tell what she was thinking. Jessie supposed it was a good thing because it gave her time to think.

Being with Ryan was everything she hadn't known she wanted and her feelings for him were growing exponentially. He was handsome, strong and kind. When she was with him, she felt herself anchored by his strength in way she'd never been with Hugh. She could learn to let go with other lovers, right? She closed her eyes because the very idea of being with anyone else was repulsive. Yet she had so much more to figure out because her fun in the sun with Ryan in the Hamptons had showed her that she and Hugh would never make it. But could she and Ryan? If he accepted a position with Black Crescent, there was no way they could ever be together.

It was so much to think about. She'd thought sleeping together would ease the tension between them, but instead it had become an ache she couldn't erase. Her emotions were complicated by the feelings Ryan evoked in her and, once they were back in reality, Jessie was going to have to figure it out one way or another.

The rest of the afternoon was a blur for Ryan. He'd made sure to keep some distance on the yacht between him and Jessie. And when they'd returned home, he hadn't joined her in the shower—no matter how much he wanted to. Their time was ending and he was preparing himself emotionally as well as physically for when they would no longer be together.

He'd succeeded.

Even after she'd come out of the bathroom, in a sexy romper for the barbecue at a friend of Dean's that evening, Ryan kept his composure despite the tug of desire in his groin. Instead, he'd slid her arm into the crook of his and led her out of the bedroom.

They joined the rest of the gang downstairs and were driven to the party on the other side of the Hamptons in a party bus big enough for eight so no one would have to drink and drive. This beach house was bigger and more grand than Adam's. After checking in at the security gate, they'd driven through a compound to an oceanfront estate.

The house was a split-level, but it was the features that stuck out in Jessie's mind. The soaring ceilings, marble floors, transom windows and coffered ceilings were miles over anything she'd ever seen. Even the O'Malley house. Partygoers were on all levels, milling around with drinks and canapés from a five-star chef in their hand.

"How did you score an invite to this?" Ryan asked Dean.

Dean shrugged. "My firm worked a big case for the owner. Invited the entire firm. Didn't think he'd mind a few extra guests."

Ryan laughed. "The more, the merrier." He tugged

Jessie's hand forward. They mixed and mingled throughout the evening, but Ryan disguised his feelings behind a wall of bravado. He made sure to keep Jessie's wineglass full, but the lady herself at a distance.

He must have been doing a good job because Adam commented when Jessie went to the ladies' room, "Everything all right with you and Jessie?"

"Yeah, why do you ask?"

"Because you've been decidedly more measured in your interactions with her today."

Ryan frowned. He was hoping no one would notice. But Adam had, which meant Jessie had, as well. "I'm taking this for what it is."

"Which is?"

"Two people having a good time."

"But that's not what you want?" Adam asked what Ryan had been trying his best not to.

"Doesn't matter what I want. Jessie has to figure out what and *who* she really wants. Not to mention, the Black Crescent job is still on the table. If I were to accept, it would cause Jessie and her family a lot of grief and tear open old wounds. So, if it seems like I'm pulling back a bit, I am. It's called self-preservation." He wasn't going to put himself out there when he wasn't sure if she felt anything for him.

"I hear you, but perhaps you should talk to her first," Adam said. "Clear the air? And far as Black Crescent goes, the job isn't a done deal yet."

Ryan grinned smugly. "Sure it is."

"A little cocky, eh?"

"More like confident," Ryan responded as he left.

The first interview had gone well and he would be called for the second any day now.

When she didn't return immediately to his side, Ryan went in search of her and found Jessie outside on the terrace looking over the beach. Despite the party around her, she seemed a million miles away. "Penny for your thoughts?"

She turned and studied him and then led with a whammy. "Why have you been avoiding me today?"

Oh, she was going straight to the point.

"I haven't been avoiding you."

She cocked her head to one side and regarded him with an angry glare. "Did you think I wouldn't feel you pulling away? Was it something I did? Are you already bored with me now that we've slept together?"

Ryan's eyes filled with horror and he placed his beer on a nearby table. He reached for her, but she stepped away from him. "Of course not. How could you think that?"

"I don't know what to feel, Ryan," she said, folding her arms across her chest in a defensive posture. "You've kept me at a distance all day."

"I'm sorry."

"Don't be sorry, for Christ's sake. Just tell me what's going on."

"I don't know how to do this." He pointed between them. "You and me."

Jessie grinned. "I beg to differ. I think you've been *doing* this quite well."

If he could have blushed, Ryan would have. "I'm not talking about how compatible we are in the bedroom. I'm talking about the fact that you're my friend and we crossed the line this weekend. And don't get me wrong, I don't regret it, Jessie." He looked into her eyes. "I wanted you. I always have. But I'm also wondering what will happen when we go back to the real world."

"I thought we were going to take this one day at a time?" Jessie asked.

"We were. I mean we are."

"I feel like you want an answer from me on what's going to happen between us after this weekend and, if I'm honest, I can't give you one. Not yet, Ryan. I'm confused about a lot of things. But what I'm not confused about is my decision to be with you this weekend."

Ryan released a heavy sigh and looked down at Jessie. The stubborn tilt of her chin as she looked into his eyes made him burn with mortification. He shouldn't have stayed away from her today. Thinking about the obstacles they faced with his possible job at Black Crescent and her family's oppressive expectations made him waste time. Plus, his pride had gotten in the way and he'd begun to think about her casting him aside to go back to Hugh. Envy that Hugh would have his woman after sharing such a passionate weekend with him had his stomach churning.

He brushed her cheek with a single finger and tucked a strand of her shoulder-length hair behind her ear. He felt her pulse quicken at his touch, because when they were together that's all it took. A spark for them to burn bright. His finger continued a path to her mouth and he marauded it back and forth over her lips. When she opened her mouth and took his finger inside and began sucking, Ryan felt his groin harden in response.

Damn minx could turn him on with the snap of her fingers. She looked up at him as she sucked his finger deep into her mouth and Ryan knew in that instant that they needed to get out of there, otherwise he would lose his grip.

He pulled away. "We need to go," he groaned hoarsely.

She nodded her agreement.

It didn't take long for them to call an Uber and say their goodbyes to the group. The short drive back to the house was fraught with sexual energy as they gave each other hungry looks. Ryan was thankful when the car came to a stop and they rushed through the front door like two randy teenagers. They quickly raced upstairs to their bedroom and began stripping, eager to get naked.

Ryan couldn't wait to please her in all kinds of ways. And he did. She trusted him to do anything and she enjoyed every minute of it. They were so amorous, they ended up on the floor, but neither of them seemed to care. After putting on protection, he allowed Jessie to sit astride his lap and set the pace.

"Take what you want," he urged her softly. "Whatever you want."

She kissed him long and deep, stroking inside his mouth with an intimate exploration. Then she lifted her hips, allowing him to slide through her feminine folds.

"Good…you feel good," he couldn't resist murmuring.

"So do you." She began rocking her hips and he tightened his arms clasping her to his chest. She rode him hard and he pushed up to meet her. Again. Then again and again. Every time she moved, he moved. She gave him everything and he claimed it. He wanted to claim all of her and when he gazed into her eyes, he could see the same sense of wonder, pleasure and need that were mirrored in his.

It wasn't just sex for her, either.

Those were his last thoughts as she feverishly clutched him, digging her fingernails into his biceps. He roared in satisfaction.

Afterward, a flash of light caught his attention. Ryan realized it was Fourth of July fireworks, but he didn't need the real-life ones because he and Jessie had made some of their own.

Nine

After a goodbye-lunch with the entire gang the following day, Jessie and Ryan headed back to Manhattan. Rather than take a helicopter to the city, Ryan had a limousine pull up to the beach house.

He was shaking Adam's hand when Tia whispered in Jessie's ear, "You've got that man around your pinky. Enjoy."

Jessie laughed as she moved toward the vehicle.

"You like?" Ryan asked.

"A limo?" Her voice rose a pitch. "Pretty fancy."

"Only the best for you."

Jessie's heart kicked over in her chest as Ryan handed her bag to the driver who'd exited the vehicle. Then he helped Jessie into the luxurious comfort of the interior and watched with amusement as she surveyed her surroundings with its plush leather seats and bottle of champagne chilling in a bucket of ice.

"Would you like a glass?" Ryan asked as the limo pulled away from the curb. They waved at the McKinleys as they left.

Jessie turned from staring out of the window. "Yes, please. A limo? Do you do this often?"

Ryan shrugged. "I often take them for business."

Jessie shook her head. "You continue to surprise me, Ryan Hathaway."

He laughed as he reached for the bottle of bubbly and popped it open. He quickly poured flutes for him and Jessie. They toasted and Jessie let the champagne course through her veins.

"I think you're sitting too far away," Ryan said as he raised the privacy glass between them and driver.

"Oh really?"

"Oh yes." Ryan took her flute from her hands and placed it next to his on the console. Then he proceeded to show Jessie that after last night and this morning's lust-filled haze, they were not nearly done with each other yet.

By the time they arrived at Jessie's brownstone after navigating the NYC traffic, they'd steamed up the windows pretty darn good.

Jessie hated to leave Ryan, but she had an early day tomorrow. She exited the limo first and Ryan joined her, helping take her bags up the stairs to her apartment.

"I had a really great time," she said awkwardly at her door. She didn't have the words to express how being with Ryan had changed her life and totally flipped the script on what happened next.

"So did I. I'll call you later."

Jessie nodded and watched as he started down the stairs, but then he must have thought better of it because he came running back up. He swooped her into his arms and pressed his mouth to hers. He took full advantage, sliding his tongue deep to taste her, tearing a soft moan from her lips. Jessie wound her arms around his neck and melted against him. Her body softened to accommodate the steel of his.

His mouth ravaged hers. How was it possible they could still be as hungry for each other when they'd just gotten busy in the back of the limo? Jessie couldn't deny that somehow Ryan had taken hold of not only her body but her soul. He'd unlocked parts of her she hadn't even been aware of.

Eventually they lifted their heads and pulled away to take in large breaths.

"Get some rest," Ryan said. "I'll call you soon." Seconds later, he was gone.

Once inside her apartment, Jessie found Becca curled up on the couch with a bowl of popcorn. "Thought I heard voices outside the door, but then when I looked through the peephole…" Becca began, "all I could see was you and Ryan going at it like rabbits."

Jessie flushed, lowered her head and began swiftly walking to her room. She could hear Becca's footsteps behind her as she followed Jessie to her bedroom.

"Don't you even dare try to hold out on me," Becca stated, flopping down on Jessie's bed. "We have seen each other through all kinds of crap. No way are you going to hold out on me that you and Ryan—*Ryan*, of all people—hooked up over the weekend."

"It wasn't a hookup," Jessie said as she emptied the majority of contents from her suitcase into the laundry hamper.

"No? Then what was it?"

Jessie shrugged. "I have no idea, Becca." She stopped unpacking. "One minute, I'm hanging out with my best friend and his friends. The next minute, I'm up against the wall and we're having the most amazing sex I've ever had in my life."

"Better than Hugh?"

"Doesn't even compare." Jessie sat beside Becca on the bed. "Ryan is…commanding and powerful when I want it and soft and gentle when I need it. He's so in tune to my every need, my every desire. I couldn't get enough of him."

"Wow! That's saying something. And this is the first time you've ever felt this connection to him?"

Jessie rose from the bed, unable to meet Becca's querying eyes. "I didn't say that."

"What does that mean? What aren't you saying?"

Jess spun around. "Three months ago at the reunion… There was a moment when Ryan and I danced that I thought there might have been a spark, but I dismissed it. Hugh came and I got caught up in the excitement of his surprise appearance."

"Clearly, you weren't wrong about that night."

Jessie nodded. "No, I don't suppose I was. This weekend was a complete revelation. I had no idea Ryan and I were so—so sexually compatible. We were together *all* weekend."

"Sounds hot! I can hardly believe it. I mean you've never once said you were interested in Ryan in that way. He was always the boy next door."

"Yeah…well, he's still that, too, but he's also got a sexy body and a wicked tongue," Jessie said with a grin. When she thought about how he used his tongue to turn her inside out, Jessie felt her skin turn crimson.

"Are you going to continue seeing him?" Becca inquired. "Isn't Ryan still applying for that job at Black Crescent?"

"Yes." Except for his friends mentioning it Friday night, Ryan hadn't spoken of the job the entire weekend. Jessie was certain that had been deliberate because they'd wanted to keep the real world out of their Hampton bubble, but it was still a real possibility.

"Could you accept him working there?"

Jessie shook her head. "I couldn't. It would hurt too much. Black Crescent cost my family everything and changed our lives forever."

"So where does that leave you? What about Hugh?"

"Hugh and I have had a long-distance relationship for years and I'm tired of it. I have been for years. We decided three months ago to take a break to figure out what we wanted."

"Why didn't you speak up and tell me sooner?"

"Because… I've always tried to do what's expected of me, what my family wants, but I'm coming to realize that it's overshadowed my life and stifled me from making my own choices."

"A choice like Ryan?"

"It's not tit for tat."

"No?"

"Of course not. I'm not using Ryan because Hugh is no longer in my life. Our attraction surprised both of us."

"Maybe you, but Ryan has always been into you, Jessie. He's always been jealous of your relationship with Hugh. You just refused to acknowledge the obvious."

"That's not true."

"It is. I knew it the moment I met him. But you'd always had him in the friend's zone and seemed content to have him there, so I never questioned it."

"Well, I'm questioning everything. So to answer your question, Ryan and I didn't really discuss what comes next once we got back home."

"What did you talk about?"

Jessie blushed. There hadn't been a whole of talking going on. Just kissing, touching, licking and lots more.

Becca fanned herself. "My apologies, my love life has been on indefinite pause. No amount of Match, eHarmony or Tinder can resuscitate it."

"You'll find someone, Becca. You're an amazing human."

"Not someone as fine as Ryan. I mean, when did he get so good-looking all of a sudden?"

Jessie chuckled. She'd thought the same thing. One day he was overweight. The next he was lean and trim and had become a man. All man. And through the years, she'd see him here and there, but she supposed she'd never really *seen* him until the reunion. And now that she had, there was no way they could go back to being only friends.

But she also wasn't sure she was ready for a full-blown relationship. There were too many obstacles she had to get through first. And they began with figuring out what she wanted and how to stop doing her parents' bidding and finally live for herself. In an ideal world, she and Ryan would be able to make their Hamptons tryst into something more, but how could they if he took the job with Black Crescent? Jessie didn't see a way forward for them and that was the most disappointing part of all.

"Well, look who the cat dragged in," Sean Hathaway, Ryan's older brother, said when Ryan joined him and their brother Ben for drinks later that evening. They were at a local pub in Murray Hill that specialized in craft beer and burgers, and was not all that far from his penthouse. He'd forgotten his brothers had come to the city after the annual Hathaway barbecue for a Yankees' game and he was to meet them beforehand for a drink.

"Don't give me a hard time," Ryan stated. "I've been busy."

"Too busy to hang out with your bros?" His younger brother, Ben stated. Ben had inherited their father's wiry frame and salt-and-pepper hair. Poor guy had started graying in his twenties. But that hadn't stopped the ladies from fawning over his light brown eyes, which was a trademark of their mother's family, even though his brother dressed like a preppie in trousers and a button-down shirt. Though tonight it appeared he'd made an exception and had traded his trousers for jeans, but still the button-down remained.

"You didn't even come home for the Fourth," Sean chimed in. "Mom was none too pleased. You know she looks forward to having us all home." His eldest brother, on the other hand, was the exact opposite of Ben. He was broad-shouldered, with a football player frame, and wore jeans and a Yankees jersey. He had dark brown hair and deeply set brown eyes.

Like Jessie's parents, Marilyn Hathaway hadn't been happy when Ryan had told her of his plans to spend the Fourth of July with his friends. His father's barbecue was one of the biggest parties on Sycamore Street and everyone in their Falling Brook neighborhood usually came out to sample Eric's ribs, brisket and pulled pork.

"Yeah, it couldn't be helped." Ryan shrugged.

"Why not?" Ben inquired. "What's so important?"

"I was hanging with some friends in the Hamptons. You remember my roommate Adam from college? He invited several of us to his place."

"By friends, do you mean Jessie Acosta?" Ben teased.

"Ah." Sean grinned and pointed at Ryan's guilty face, "Now that makes sense. There's only one person that would make Ryan abandon his family and that would be a certain beautiful Latina."

"Don't start," Ryan admonished.

"Tease you about the crush you've had on the girl next door for decades?" Sean stated, wrapping his arm around Ryan's shoulder. "No way, bro. You've got it coming and then some. I'm friends with Jessie on Facebook. I saw the pictures she posted. You can't hide the look of absolute adoration on your face."

Ryan rolled his eyes. "Adoration? That was in the past. I stopped pining for Jessie months ago when I realized at the reunion that she was never going to choose me."

"Yet you took her with you to the Hamptons?" Sean quipped.

"That was different. It was just a temporary fling."

Both his brothers laughed, but it was Ben who piped up next. "You're so sprung on that girl. Always have been and always will be."

"Agreed," Sean stated. "But what was more interesting about the pics posted was the look in her eyes." Sean pulled out his IPhone and showed a picture of Ryan and Jessie with his friends. "Finally, after all these years, little Jessie is feeling you. Isn't that right?"

Ryan rose from the high-top table they were seated at and moved over to the bar. He motioned to the bartender and quickly ordered a beer. He needed a minute to collect himself before he faced his brothers. If anyone could read him, they could. He didn't want them to know how much he wanted that to be true. How much he wanted Jessie to be as into him as he was into her.

The bartender slid a beer across the bar and Ryan accepted it, taking a swig. When he returned to the table, his brothers eyed him.

"Well?" Sean asked. "Are you going to fess up now? Or are we going to have to beat it out of you?" He glanced at Ben who nodded his agreement. When Ryan was younger, his older brothers loved razzing him.

Ben held up his hand. "I vote to beat it out of him. It's been a while since we gave our little brother a proper whooping."

"As if you could take me," Ryan snorted. "I'm not that chubby kid you guys could push around. Like Popeye, I've been eating my spinach," He showed off his biceps "And I can take either of you. Any time of day."

Sean threw back his head and roared with laughter. "Is that right? You are definitely full of yourself because Jessie Acosta finally gave you the time of day."

"C'mon, spill," Ben said, staring at Ryan.

"I admit I invited Jessie to the Hamptons with me and our relationship went to the next level."

"Okay, I want my twenty bucks." Sean held out his hand to Ben.

Ryan glanced at his brothers. "Did you guys make a bet on me and Jessie?" he asked incredulously.

"Sure did," Sean said as Ben pulled out a twenty-dollar bill and handed it to him. He tucked the money into his jeans. "I told Ben that Jessie finally opened her eyes to what's been right in front of her the entire time. He told me no way. He was wrong."

"How could you tell?" Ryan asked. "That picture was of all of us at the party."

"Yeah, but if you look real close, you can see your hand was around her waist, real proprietary-like, and you had a look of absolute happiness," Sean replied. "So, are you happy?"

Ryan took a swig of beer. "Why wouldn't I be?"

"Because you're here with us instead of your new lady love," Ben responded.

Ryan laughed at his euphemism. "It's a bit early to start calling her my lady."

"Well, she's certainly not O'Malley's anymore," Sean said with a smirk.

Ryan frowned. Hearing his nemesis's name always irked him.

"I don't want to talk about Hugh."

"Why not?" Ben asked. "He's been your competition from the start to win Jessie. Is he out of the picture?"

Ryan shrugged. "I think so."

"But you don't know for sure?" Sean finished.

Ryan shook his head. And that bothered him. He didn't know exactly where Jessie stood with Hugh or anything. She'd said they were on a break, but Ryan wasn't so sure. Hugh was still formidable opposition standing in the way of his finding true happiness with Jessie. There was also the possible job at Black Crescent to contend with.

"You need to find out," Sean stated. "You can't stay in limbo. I know how you've felt…" he began and then corrected himself. "How you *feel* about Jessie. You should have an honest heart-to-heart talk and find out where you stand."

Ryan put down his beer and looked at both his brothers. "In due time." He didn't want to fall back into bad habits, not after he'd done such a good job of pushing down his feelings after the reunion. He didn't want to take a step back.

"All right, but that's the only way you'll have your answer," Ben said. "If it doesn't work out, you'll have the memories to look back on about your one hot week-end together in the Hamptons."

Ryan frowned. He didn't like Ben's honest assess-ment, but he knew his brother was right. He and Jessie needed to clear the air and come to an understanding. He needed to know if what they shared was just a fling for her. Because it sure as hell wasn't for him. He'd begun thinking of the end game because, in his mind, he wanted her to be Mrs. Ryan Hathaway.

Ten

Ryan was in a bad mood. After getting up at 5:00 a.m. to complete his workout regime to keep his body fit and trim, he'd checked the overnight news to see if there were any relevant market movements. Finding none, he prepared himself for the firm's morning meeting. He had some investment ideas he wanted to discuss with upper management before making a presentation to his institutional clients.

The morning meeting went as expected and they loved his ideas. So he'd gone back to his office to set up appointments, including an investor visit to a distribution center. The only bright spot had been Allison Randall, the recruitment specialist, calling him to advise Black Crescent was interviewing other candidates, but was very happy with him and she hoped to have the second interview set up shortly. Ryan had expected as much. His credentials spoke for themselves.

Yet by midmorning, Ryan still felt unsettled and he knew why. After sharing brews and burgers with his brothers last night, he'd gone home full of purpose and expecting to have a serious conversation with Jessie about the state of their relationship. Instead, all he'd gotten was silence. His calls, voice mails and texts had gone unanswered for the entire evening.

If Jessie was trying to tell him what happened in the Hamptons stayed in the Hamptons, he'd received the message loud and clear. He supposed he shouldn't be surprised, it had been her idea to keep the weekend light and strings-free. He'd gone along because he'd wanted her so badly, he'd been willing to compromise. When in fact, he wanted it all—marriage and babies— with Jessie.

He knew to tell her would be suicide and send her running in the opposite direction. But at the very least, he'd hoped she'd want to continue seeing him to see where they might lead.

He'd been wrong.

Instead, he'd gotten his hopes up only to have them dashed and he had no one to blame but himself.

"Hey, Ryan, would you mind looking at some of my research?" Mark Bush, a junior analyst at his firm, said from his doorway.

"Of course." Ryan motioned him inside. He liked the kid. He was young, straight out of Trinity and a little green, but he had tremendous promise. Ryan wasn't like some of the other senior analysts who treated those underneath him like the bottom of their shoe, making them work hard like an intern. He believed in paying it forward.

Ryan peered over the figures Mark presented. "These are good. Really good."

"Thanks, Ryan. I appreciate you taking a look."

Ryan smiled. "You're welcome."

Helping others had always brought Ryan joy, which was why he wanted to run Black Crescent Investment. The company had bounced back under Joshua Lowell's leadership, but if Ryan became CEO, he was certain he could get rid of the tarnished reputation once and for all. Many in Falling Brook thought the Lowells were still secretly in contact with Vernon. That's why Ryan felt he was the right choice to lead the company.

With someone new at the helm, the fund wouldn't be accused of financial malfeasance and could finally be the leader in investments it had once been.

Black Crescent, however, wasn't Ryan's only opportunity to move into upper management. He was pursuing a couple of other interesting initiatives—though none of them had the personal impact of working in his hometown. Working at Black Crescent had been Ryan's way of cutting ties with Jessie and exorcising her from his life *permanently*.

Maybe he'd been onto something a few months ago. Jessie's lack of communication was a blessing to show him he needed to focus on himself and his career. Or at least, that's what he told himself as he continued working until the sky darkened outside.

"You still here?" Mark said.

Ryan glanced up from the report he'd been reading. It's not like he had anyone to go home to. "Yeah, I'll be here for a while. I'll see you tomorrow."

"Sure thing. Have a good night."

Ryan returned to studying the facts and figures in front of him until a silhouette at the door captured his attention. He sucked in a deep breath.

Jessie.

Jessie stared into Ryan's dark brown eyes and let out a sigh of relief. It had been too long to go without seeing him. She'd had every intention of calling him last night, but after drinking a couple of glasses of wine with Becca, she'd drifted off to sleep and hadn't awakened until Becca alerted her she'd overslept because her phone was dead.

She'd barely had enough time to shower before catching the subway to work—leaving her phone at home on the charger. Jessie hadn't realized how exhausted she'd been from the weekend, but she supposed it was because she'd stayed in bed with *this man* and hadn't gotten much sleep.

Though she didn't like the frown currently marring his features. "Ryan, listen… I'm sorry," she began as she walked into his office and shut the door.

"What for?" he asked, closing the folder he'd obviously been reading.

"Because I told you we'd talk last night and I fell asleep."

"And this morning?" he queried. "Heck, the rest

of the day, for that matter. You mean to tell me, you couldn't bother to pick up a phone?"

"I overslept and left my phone at home, and you know I'm terrible with remembering numbers. That's your forte not mine."

He eyed her suspiciously, as if he didn't quite believe her, and a funny ache began to develop in her chest. She wasn't used to Ryan being this cold toward her and she didn't like it. Not one bit.

"C'mon…" She tossed her purse and briefcase on the chair in front of his desk and walked around to sit on top of his desk. "Don't be mad. I really did mean to call you, but I was exhausted and, quite frankly, it's all your fault."

"My fault?"

"If you hadn't kept me awake for nearly three nights straight, I might have gotten some rest."

Her statement finally produced a smile and the pain in her chest began to subside.

"All right. Well, you're here now…what did you want to talk about?" Ryan asked.

"Talk?" Jessie said with a grin. Standing, she sashayed over to the door and locked it. She was thankful his office wasn't all glass or had a sidelight. They would have all the privacy they needed for what she had in mind. "I wasn't exactly thinking about talking."

"Oh really?"

"Oh yes. I'm sure there's another activity we could come up with." She walked back to him and, before he could move, she covered his mouth with hers. The kiss was every bit as ravaging as it always was between them. Tongues seeking, tasting, taking everything. Jessie hadn't thought about what she would say when she'd come to Ryan's office. She'd assumed they would discuss their future. But when she'd seen the frown on his face and obvious displeasure with her, she knew one way to put him in a better frame of mine.

She'd thought she would be in control of the situation, but she quickly found out she was wrong as his fingers deftly unfastened the buttons on her pink silk blouse and tossed it to the floor. "Ryan…" she began, but he was already disposing of her black bra to expose her breasts.

"I thought we weren't talking," he said, quickly spinning her around so she was bent over his desk.

Any thought of her being the one to establish the rules and boundaries of their affair quickly vanished when his roving hands were everywhere. When he came to the hem of her black pencil skirt, he pushed under and up. His warm palm slid across her buttocks and over the panel of her thong. Jessie trembled and her breathing quickened when he began kissing her neck and his fingers rubbed the place where she ached for his touch.

But he didn't reward her with what she wanted. Instead, he tipped her head back and his tongue plundered the cavern of her mouth. He was dominant and claiming her, and Jessie yielded to the passion he evoked in her. She wanted him. *Now.*

"Please." She knew she was begging, but she had no control when she was with Ryan.

Ryan's fingers pushed the silk scrap of material aside to probe her damp, hot sex. Jessie gasped as delicious sensations curled through her. She arched into his erection and shamelessly rubbed her bottom against him, desperate to get off. That only seemed to aggravate him and she heard the rip of material, rustle of a packet and the tug of his zipper. Then he was there. Right there. Nudging her thighs apart and surging inside her.

Their lovemaking was wilder and hotter than anything Jessie could imagine. She was bent over and Ryan was holding her hips while he established a devastatingly fast, hard rhythm that had her moaning in pleasure as any element of control she thought she had was shattered. And when Ryan thrust again, his harsh groan was mingled with her orgasm as they both climaxed together.

Afterward, he spun her in his arms and claimed her mouth in a slow, deeply sensual kiss that made what they'd shared even more profound.

When their breathing finally returned to normal, Ryan pulled away to discard the protection, asking, "Was it good for you?"

Jessie smiled as she rebuttoned her blouse and pulled down her skirt. The thong, lying in tatters on the floor, meant she would have to go without underwear, which felt even more sinful. "What do you think?"

"I hope I wasn't…"

She blushed. She'd never been as uninhibited as she was than when they were together. "You were just right."

After zipping up, Ryan sat in his chair and pulled Jessie into his lap. "I suppose we should have that talk now."

"You mean the one where I was going to tell you I wanted to see where this goes? You mean that one?"

His face lit up as if he'd won the Super Bowl. "Yeah, that one."

Jessie stroked his cheek with her palm. "I like you, Ryan. I think you know that. I like you a lot and I'm not exactly sure where this is leading, but I'd like to find out."

He grasped both sides of her face and brushed his lips across hers. "So would I. So would I."

Eleven

Ryan couldn't believe he and Jessie were an item. They weren't exactly boyfriend and girlfriend, but they'd definitely crossed the threshold of being more than just lovers. He'd been so angry when he'd thought she'd stood him up, but then she'd come to his office to apologize. His emotions had been somewhat high if the way he'd taken her from behind on his desk was any indication.

However, what came after was even more precious. After packing a bag at her apartment, much to Becca's obvious approval, Jessie had returned to his penthouse that evening and had rarely left since. And that had been two weeks ago.

They'd both agree to keep their relationship private and to not tell either of their parents. Ryan's motives were clear because he didn't want the Hathaways getting their hopes up until he was sure exactly where they were headed. Jessie's parents, he wasn't so sure of. Was she still not ready to stand up to them and all their expectations to tell them she'd made a decision for herself and chosen Ryan over Hugh? That rankled him.

Ryan wanted Jessie to say she was completely done with Hugh, but he supposed it was hard, given she'd been with the man for over a decade. He was having to exercise patience when it came to Jessie. He didn't want to move too fast or to rush her into something she would later regret.

Instead, he was enjoying how easy it was for them to be together. After work, they'd usually congregate on the sofa with their laptops and work. He'd whip up dinner in his superb chef's kitchen, which was outfitted with a Bosch electric cooktop stove, Fisher & Paykel refrigerator and microwave, and chrome appliances. He was a pretty good cook having learned to survive after college.

Sometimes they sat out on his private terrace with a glass of wine. Other times, they'd get takeout and catch a Netflix movie on his built-in concealed television on the wall and make love until the wee hours of the morning until they were both spent yet fully satisfied.

Their relationship wasn't always sunshine and roses. They'd argued once when she'd heard him calling Allison Randall for an update on scheduling his second interview with Black Crescent. Jessie had made it very clear she was vehemently opposed, but then she'd backed down when he'd told her he had no news to report. Ryan knew it was just a matter time before they both had to take a stand, but he was enjoying their relationship until then.

One day last week, he'd surprised her with front-row Broadway tix that one of his clients had given him. But tonight, Ryan had planned something special.

He would whisk her away to an enchanted garden for a private dinner. He'd arranged it with a friend who had a membership at the garden. A client of his, Theo Morales, was a local chef who owned a farm-to-table restaurant and he was preparing a feast for them to enjoy. Ryan was already dressed for the casual evening in dark jeans and a black button-down sport shirt.

When Jessie arrived at his penthouse that evening, she was still dressed in a suit and wearing heels. Her usually straight hair had started to wave up because of the humidity from the hot July evening.

"Hey, babe." Ryan took her briefcase from her and handed her a glass of wine.

"Thank you," Jessie said, kicking off her heels and plopping down on his leather sectional. "It's been a long day. I'm so glad we can just kick back and relax."

"Actually—" he sat beside her on the sofa "—I was thinking we could go out tonight."

Jessie glanced at him. "Do we have to? I was hoping for a quiet evening in."

"We do. It's nothing fancy. But I promise you, you'll enjoy."

She eyed him suspiciously.

"Trust me."

After showering, Jessie changed into slim-fitting jeans, which had Ryan salivating at her pert bottom, a floral-print blouse and espadrilles. He could tell she'd flat-ironed her hair because it was back to being bone-straight. She looked cute and sexy as hell, but then again, he always thought that. Although it had taken them a long time to go from friends to lovers to a couple, it was so natural and felt so right, it was like it was always meant to be. He didn't want to think that it could all go away if he accepted the job at Black Crescent.

"You ready?" he asked, snatching his phone and wallet off the console table.

"I am, but I'm curious as to where you're taking me."

"You'll see." Ryan grabbed her hand and they took the elevator down to the first floor. A cab, waiting outside, whisked them away to the East Village to the Sixth Street and Avenue B Community Garden.

When the cab pulled up outside the black wrought-iron gates, Jessie turned to look at him. "What's going on?"

"Wait for it." He paid the cabbie and slid out of the backseat to stand on the pavement and helped Jessie from the cab. Theo was waiting for him at the entrance.

"Ryan!" Theo grabbed his hand and pulled him into a one-armed hug. "It's good to see you. Welcome to 6 & B Garden."

"Thank you, Theo. This is my lady—" he circled his arm around Jessie's waist and pulled her forward "—Jessie Acosta."

Theo grasped her hand and placed it to his lips. "A pleasure." He released her hand and looked at Ryan. "Are you ready for a feast for the senses?"

"Absolutely." Ryan smiled, glancing down at Jessie. "Lead the way."

Theo opened the gate and led them through a maze of ornamental shrubs and lush evergreen trees, past the garden plots for many of its members. On the way, Theo pointed out the different variety of fruiting trees, flowering shrubs and innumerable herbs, flowers and vegetables.

"This is amazing," Jessie said. "And the members keep this all up?"

"Year-round," Theo commented. "But now we're part of a nonprofit corporation comprised of a board of directors, many of whom are garden members, along with some community leaders. Everyone wants to lend their expertise and support, and because of that we've been going strong for decades."

"I never knew," Jessie commented.

"Wait to see what your man has in store for you."

Several minutes later, they'd come to a beautiful decorated trellis with string lights, lanterns and large urns of colorful seasonal flowers everywhere. And in the middle of it all was a candlelight dinner for two.

"Well, what do you think?"

Jessie was overcome. She couldn't believe Ryan had gone to all this trouble for a Wednesday night date. They'd been spending so much time together, she hadn't spent much of the last weeks in her own bed. She hadn't wanted to be separated from him—and that scared her. Was she getting in over her head? She'd pretty much ignored calls from her folks in Falling Brook and Hugh in London. She was sure they all wanted to know what was going on and hoping things would return to normal. But they wouldn't. Couldn't. At first, she'd felt guilty for abandoning her family, but for the first time in her life, Jessie felt free and liberated. Able to do what she wanted and be damned with what her parents or anyone else thought about it.

Instead, she and Ryan had only grown closer. They spoke everyday on the phone whenever she could take a break at work and texted often. And at night…well, that was off the charts. Ryan made love to her with such passion. He knew her body so intimately, probably better than Jessie ever did.

And now he'd done this. Something so romantic but yet completely Ryan. "Thank you. I love it." She couldn't resist smiling from ear to ear.

"Come." Ryan held out the chair for her. She sat and he joined her, sitting across from her. A large cloche covered both place settings.

"I've quite the meal planned for you lovebirds," Theo stated, "but for now, enjoy the salad, straight from the garden." He lifted both their domes. "It's a shaved trumpet mushroom salad with a truffle vinaigrette. Hope you enjoy." He quickly left the area, leaving them alone.

"Ryan, how did you manage this?" Jessie said, glancing around. "It's magnificent."

He shrugged. "I rented the garden out for the night so we could have privacy and enjoy the surroundings."

Jessie's heart sang with delight and she blinked away the tears at the backs of her eyes. "Thank you. No one has ever done anything like this for me."

His gaze met hers and traveled over her face, searching her eyes. "You deserve it, Jessie. I hope you know how much the last couple of weeks have meant to me. And I wanted to do something meaningful."

She nodded, overcome with emotion. "You did. You did."

The rest of their dinner was nothing short of superb. Theo went all-out with the second course of duck à l'orange with glazed turnips picked straight from the garden. The dessert was a delicious lemon meringue tart with a compote made from the fruits in the garden. Jessie dabbed her napkin at the sides of her mouth.

"Theo, dinner was magnificent. Thank you so much."

"You're welcome. I hope we'll see you both soon?" He glanced at Ryan. "Maybe at our next public event we're hosting?"

"We definitely won't be a stranger," Ryan said and looked over at Jessie. "Care for a stroll?"

"Would love one."

They took a leisurely walk through the gardens, taking time to admire the different species of plants and vegetables while smelling flowering lilacs and sunflowers. When they ended back up at the front gates, Jessie stopped and spun into Ryan's arms. She tilted her head back and pressed her lips against his. He grasped her to him, claiming her lips languidly as if they had all the time in the world, as if she belonged to him. And she did because with each stroke of his tongue, Jessie couldn't bear to tear herself away from him.

Eventually, Ryan lifted his head. "Let's get back to my place," he murmured.

"Yes."

Jessie didn't remember the cab ride to Ryan's. All she could think about was getting Ryan alone and naked. Naked being the operative word. As soon as they were in his private elevator, riding to his penthouse, they were all over each other, kissing and touching. When the elevator dinged, they didn't even separate, they just continued kissing.

Shoes were kicked off and shirts began flying everywhere, followed by their jeans. By the time they reached Ryan's bedroom, there was a trail of clothes behind them, but they were both thankfully naked. They joined together with such intensity in a mass of limbs on the bed that Jessie felt she would pass out from the excitement. Instead, she heard a purring sound in her throat when Ryan slid inside her and they became one. She writhed, clinging to him as the entire world fell away and Ryan was her anchor. When their release came, Ryan shouted and Jessie cried out because they'd reached paradise and it had never felt so good.

Those were her last thoughts as she drifted off to sleep.

Could life get any better? Although Ryan hadn't heard any more about the Black Crescent opportunity, he knew he was still in the running, so he was taking it one day at a time. He also knew that, at some point, he would have to make a decision, but for now he was enjoying the ride. He was discovering new things about

Jessie each day. She was breaking out of her parents' shadow and doing what was best for her.

It was an attractive quality, Ryan thought the next evening when he and Jessie attended one of his favorite activities. They were volunteering at a local school's food bank, stocking shelves with peanut butter, jelly, canned goods and snacks. After learning many children didn't eat after they left school, Ryan had wanted to get involved and had been donating money as well as giving his time to help stock groceries for children to take home with them for the weekend.

Ryan's special treat last night had really touched Jessie and she'd showed her appreciation when they'd gotten home. Ryan smiled when he thought about her hands and mouth on him. He'd thought he'd worn her out and, with her hard day at work, he'd assumed she'd want to stay in tonight. Instead, she agreed to accompany him.

"Why wouldn't I come? Do you think I'm that much of a diva?"

"Of course not," Ryan replied. "You've never talked about giving back, is all."

"I should," Jessie replied. "Our family was one paycheck away from needing their services after Black Crescent went bust. We almost left Falling Brook and moved in with my grandparents in Brooklyn."

"I'm glad that day never came," Ryan said.

"It wasn't easy. Although my dad was employed after the crash, ultimately, it was my mother who put in long hours at the dealership, often working overtime until eventually she was made office manager."

"Does she resent your father for never recovering from the disaster?"

Jessie stopped filling up the food bag and looked at him. "That's a fair question, but one I've never asked her. My parents' marriage has always been somewhat of a mystery to me."

"Why is that?"

"They sleep in separate rooms. She has her job and clubs, while he stays at home and broods. I've always wondered why they're still together. I suppose it led to my trying to be helpful after Black Crescent collapsed. I just wanted them to be happy again and they were when my exposure to the O'Malleys led me to date Hugh. And so I've continued fulfilling their expectations for my life and future, but I've been unhappy and dissatisfied for a long time. I want what your parents have. I've never seen two people as in love with each other as your parents are."

Ryan smiled. "Thank you." He was proud his parents had celebrated thirty-five years of marriage and were still going strong. He wanted to emulate them and have the same kind of solid foundation they had one day. "Speaking of my family… My mom's birthday is coming up this weekend. I know we said we'd keep our relationship between us, but I'd really like it if you could make it."

Jessie's brow quirked questioningly. "Are you sure I should come to a *family* gathering? I mean… I haven't spent time with your mother in years. Won't she suspect something?"

"You're still my friend. There's no reason you can't join us, if you 'happen' to be in town."

"I don't know."

"C'mon, it'll be fun. And I'd really like to have you there."

"If I go, I'll have to stay at my parents'," Jessie said. "There's no way I could come home and not make an appearance. My mother would roast me over the coals."

"Of course."

They continued boxing and bagging up groceries for the school, but in the back of his mind Ryan knew that any day now, when his second Black Crescent interview was called, their relationship could come tumbling down.

Jessie didn't know why she was nervous as she sat in the passenger seat of Ryan's Porsche 911 Carrera as he drove them to Falling Brook for the weekend. It wasn't like he hadn't given her a lift before, but this time was different. They were an unofficial couple and hadn't yet shared this detail with any of their friends or family, except Becca and Adam.

This weekend would be the first time she accompanied him to a public outing where his family and anyone else in the community would see them. Was she afraid of the blowback? Absolutely. Although she and Hugh were on a break, she didn't want to hurt him, either, and if anyone gossiped about her and Ryan being together, he could feel betrayed.

Not that she owed him anything. She'd been honest nearly four months ago when she'd shared with him that their decade-old, long-distance relationship wasn't working. They were on two different paths. But she wasn't looking forward to her parents' disappointment on learning that she and Hugh were no longer an item. Sometimes the weight of living up to their dreams was almost too much to bear.

"You okay?" Ryan asked, reaching for her hand from across the gearshift. "Your hands are like ice. Are you nervous about coming home?"

She shook her head in denial.

"Liar."

She turned to face him. *How could he tell?*

"I'm one of your oldest friends, do you think I can't tell when you have something on your mind? Anyway, you're like me—you're very expressive and whatever you are thinking shows on your face."

"You know me so well. And yes, I'm a bit nervous, but not about your family."

"About yours? Hugh's?"

She nodded. He'd hit the nail on the head.

"We agreed to take this as slow as you need," Ryan said.

"I know. It's not easy coming back here sometimes. All the expectations and obligations overwhelm me."

He squeezed her hand. "Don't let it. You have me and I'll protect you."

She couldn't resist smiling at him, because Ryan did have a way of easing her anxiety. He'd always been a shoulder she could lean on, the man who listened to her troubles without judging her. "I'm extremely lucky to have you."

He kissed the back of her hand and then released her as he pulled into the Falling Brook city limits. They passed the coffee shop, dry cleaner's and post office on the way to oak-tree lined Sycamore Street. Jessie's anxiety increased when they passed O'Malley Luxury Motors and she had to remind herself to breathe.

Finally, Ryan pulled into her parents' paved driveway. Her family's five-bedroom home was once the talk of the neighborhood with its traditional Spanish red-tiled roof, wrought-iron work and manicured lawn. But over the years, newer more modern homes had been built, making theirs a shadow of what it once was.

She hopped out of the car without waiting for Ryan. Her mother's Maserati was in the driveway, so she wanted to beat her to the punch before she came out to meet them. "Thanks for the ride."

"Jessie, for Christ's sake, relax!" Ryan exclaimed as he walked around to the trunk to get her bag. "I can walk you to the door without your parents or anyone else for that matter seeing alarm bells."

Jessie offered a tentative smile. "I'm sorry."

The front door opened and her mother did exactly as she thought and rushed to greet them, launching herself at Jessie. "Honey, I'm so glad you're home. It's been ages."

Angela Acosta matched Jessie in height. Her complexion was fairer than Jessie's, but they shared the same jet-black hair and small curves as many of their ancestors. "It's only been a few weeks," Jessie replied, pulling back. "Mama, you remember Ryan."

"Ryan!" her mother exclaimed and came forward

to wrap him in her embrace. "How are you? Now, you haven't been home in a while. Your mother was sorry you couldn't join her for their annual Fourth of July barbecue. My Jessie couldn't, either."

Jessie glanced at Ryan and they both had to resist a smirk.

"Well, I'm here now, Mrs. Acosta. We're celebrating Mom's birthday." Ryan handed Jessie her bag. "I'll see you later."

Jessie couldn't resist watching Ryan walk away. She waved as he got back into his car and drove to the house next door.

"It was so nice of Ryan to bring you home this weekend." Her mother grasped her by the arm and led her inside.

"We've been getting close again," Jessie said once they were indoors and she'd dropped her bag in the foyer.

"That's wonderful, dear," her mother said, releasing her arm. "And you're sure Hugh won't have a problem with that?"

Jessie frowned, folding her arms across her chest. "Why would he? Ryan and I are friends."

Her mother shrugged. "I don't know. You know what they say—men and women are rarely just friends."

"You and Mr. O'Malley are," Jessie commented. "You've been working for him for years and he's always been so kind to us. Helping me and Pete stay at Falling Brook Prep."

Jessie was surprised to see her mother blush, "Uh, yes, we have been friends—I mean colleagues for some time."

Was her mother flustered? Her skin had become pink

and Jessie could see the entire topic was making her uncomfortable.

"Is that you, buttercup?" Her father's voice rang out.

"Yes, it's me, Daddy." Following the sound of his voice, Jessie found him in the living room watching a golf tournament. She frowned when she saw a glass of brown liquid beside him. Plastering a smile on her face, Jessie walked over to give her father a kiss.

"It's good to see you, sweetheart." Her father had been her hero. Well under six feet, Peter Acosta was normally average weight, but it looked as if he'd dropped some pounds recently. And his once jet-black hair, like her own, had grayed at the temples. He'd also grown a salt-and-pepper beard since the last time she'd seen him. And why was he still in his pajamas in the afternoon?

"You, too, Daddy. I thought while we were home we could go to the golf range and you could help me with driving?" She knew how much he'd enjoyed the sport before he'd been kicked out of the country club for non-payment of dues.

As soon as she'd made enough in the firm, she'd paid for a membership for him again, but her father adamantly refused it. He didn't take handouts, certainly not from his daughter. Furthermore, he didn't want to hang around fake people who ditched their friends. Because that's exactly what had happened to her parents. Friends they'd known and socialized with for years had ostracized him and made him feel small after the loss of their wealth.

"Oh, I don't think so," Pete Acosta replied. "I could never go back there."

"We don't have to go the country club, Daddy. A fun spot just opened in the nearby town. It's called Top Golf. You can practice your swing on their range. It even shows replays and your stats on the display, which helps you make adjustments to your swing. What do you say?"

"I say it sounds like a lot of fun, Pete." Her mother concurred, patting his shoulder, which was the most contact Jessie had seen from her mother toward him in years. Why had she not noticed it before? Was it because she and Ryan were so affectionate and touched each other often? "Did you ask your brother and Amanda if they could join us?"

"Already on it. I couldn't get reservations for tonight…" Jessie added because once she told her mother she was going out with Ryan, it was going to be a big deal. "So I made them for tomorrow. Could be a family affair. What do you say?"

Her father smiled. "It sounds wonderful, buttercup. Thank you."

Jessie released a sigh of relief. She would get her father away from the television and finally living again with the rest of the world. She wanted to do the right thing for her family, but for them that meant salvaging her relationship with Hugh, even when Jessie's heart was starting to lead her in a different direction.

"How's my baby boy," Marilyn Hathaway said when Ryan had come strolling into the family home minutes earlier. His mother was in the kitchen baking his favorite chocolate-chip cookies.

Ryan swiped one as he swept his mother into a whirlwind hug. "Good now that I see you. You're as beautiful as ever."

"Oh stop!" She patted his chest. "And put me down."

He did as instructed and continued munching the cookie in his mouth. "Have Sean and Ben arrived?"

"Ben and Daphne are on their way. Sean and Monica will be along shortly. Monica had a bout of morning sickness, so they'll be a bit behind." His sister-in-law, Monica, although past her first trimester, was still suffering during her pregnancy.

"That means I get you all to myself," Ryan said, reaching for another cookie.

"I don't mind that at all," his mother replied. "So tell me what's new with you? Seems like we haven't chatted much the last few weeks." Ryan and his mother were close and usually spoke a couple of times a week, but since Jessie, his attentions had been focused elsewhere.

"Um, that's because I've been real busy."

His mother folded her arms across her chest. "Do I look stupid? A young woman has turned your head and that's who you're spending all your time with."

Ryan chuckled. "Mom, that's getting awful personal."

"And since when do you have a problem telling me you're dating?" she inquired. "Unless—" she paused and eyed him "—you think this one is someone special? Someone you could get serious with?"

"Aww, Mom. Don't go marrying me off just yet. I'm still in my twenties. There's plenty of time."

"That's what you young folks always think." His

father, Eric, joined them in the kitchen. "How are you son?" He gave Ryan a one-armed hug.

"I'm good, Dad. You're looking well."

"That's because I have your mom by my side and she takes good care of your old man." He flashed his wife a smile.

His father was the picture of health. He'd been diagnosed with Type II diabetes and had to adjust his diet, losing thirty pounds in the process. Over six feet tall, his father now looked slim and trim in the Nike tracksuit he wore. They were similar in that Ryan and his father had the same brown complexion. "You need a good woman by your side."

"Just because Sean and Ben have coupled up doesn't mean I'm ready to join in."

"But you are seeing someone?" his mother inquired. When she wanted something, she could be persistent.

"Yes."

"I knew it." His mother pointed her spatula at him as she took another tray of cookies out of the oven. This time they were peanut butter, Sean's favorite. She spoiled him and his brothers rotten, always making treats when they were home. "A mother knows these things."

"How's that job opportunity with Black Crescent coming along?" his father inquired.

Ryan's brow furrowed. He was hoping to not have to think about it because he knew it would draw a line in the sand in his relationship with Jessie. "Slowly, Dad. Black Crescent's interview process is moving at a snail's pace. I know I'm not the only candidate, but you would think I would have heard something by now."

"Are you sure you want to move back to town?" his mother inquired. "You've lived in Manhattan since you left home."

"I know. I wanted a change of scenery."

"It's your choice," his father said, "and we'd love to have you close by. But be sure you can live with the decision. Black Crescent caused this community and the Acostas, our neighbors, a lot of heartache. I know Joshua Lowell has done a lot to fix things, but to some people it will never be enough."

"I will, Dad," Ryan replied because, quite honestly, he was having a hard time justifying his reasoning for choosing Black Crescent. At the time, it had seemed like the right choice to put distance between him and Jessie. But the more time he spent with Jessie, the more Ryan realized the company played a huge role in shaping her life. Could he live with himself if he was the cause of Jessie backsliding and going back to living by her family's expectations?

Twelve

"I can't believe you're leaving us to spend time with Ryan and his family," her mother wailed. "I thought you were here to be with *your* family."

"Oh, Angela, don't make the girl feel bad," her father stated. "It's one night and she's been with us all day, helping you in your garden."

"I know that, Pete, but we get to see her so infrequently."

"It's only a few hours. I'll be back in no time. It's Mrs. Hathaway's sixtieth birthday." Jessie had already texted Ryan to meet her outside.

"I didn't know you were close with the Hathaways anymore."

Jessie didn't bother commenting. "I'll see you later. Don't wait up." She waved and quickly left the house.

She didn't want any more comments or questions from her mother. No, she hadn't been close with Ryan's mother for some time, but she was *very close* to Ryan and it meant a lot to him that she came tonight.

She'd dressed with care for the evening, choosing a little black spaghetti-strapped dress with hints of silver, which hit below the knee. It was the perfect complement to the black suit and silver tie Ryan planned to wear. Modest makeup, silver earrings, kitten heels and a black clutch completed her look. Jessie was satisfied Mrs. Hathaway would not have a problem with her ensemble.

Walking the short distance between driveways, Jessie was nearly to the Hathaway house when an arm encircled her waist, bringing her into the shadows.

"Ryan..."

She didn't get another word out because he cupped her face in his hands and kissed her. She wound her arms around his neck and opened her lips to his invading tongue. He plundered her mouth, kissing her deeply and reminding her of exactly what he could do to her. Make her on fire for him so that every part of her was hungry for more contact.

Ryan pulled back. "Easy, love."

"Then don't start something you don't plan to finish," Jessie replied with a groan.

"I'm sorry. I missed you," Ryan whispered.

"So did I." And she had. Because Ryan made her feel special. So special, it scared her. Could this be real? She'd never felt this closeness with Hugh or even with her own family.

"C'mon." He grabbed her hand to lead her inside, but Jessie stopped him.

"No." She wrenched her hand a way. "You've just kissed me senseless. I need a moment to repair the damage to my makeup." She pulled her compact and lipstick out of her purse and quickly touched up her face. When she was done, she said, "Now I'm ready."

Jessie took his breath away.

Ryan was certain his entire family could see how absolutely he'd fallen for her. Tonight she'd sparkled. His parents hadn't said a word when he'd brought Jessie into the house. Instead, his mother had enveloped her in a warm hug and welcomed her back into the fold.

Soon his brothers, in black tie, arrived with their wives and they'd all hopped into the limousine Ryan had procured to take them to the country club where they were to have dinner.

He knew his mother didn't like big displays of wealth, but this was different. It was her sixtieth birthday and she'd already done so much for him and his brothers, they'd all agreed she deserved something nice for her birthday.

They enjoyed a glass of champagne on the drive to the country club and once there, were led into a private dining room where the chef had prepared a special menu for his mother.

"Honey, you didn't have to go to all this trouble," his mother said, looking at Ryan. *How did she manage to know he was the instigator of the plan?* Like she'd always known when they were up to no good. Once, he and Ben had been playing ball in the house and broken her favorite lamp. They'd tried to superglue it and hoped she wouldn't notice. But Marilyn Hathaway had known instantly and they'd gotten the punishment to prove it. A week without video games.

"You're worth it, Mom," Ryan replied.

"I'm happy to have all my boys here," she said, glancing around the room. "And my daughters." She glanced at her daughters-in-law and then at Jessie. "You, too, Jessie."

Ryan felt Jessie clutch his hand from underneath the table. He could see she was touched by his mother's words.

The dinner went exactly as planned. The food was delicious, and his mother was genuine happily to be surrounded by her sons and their women. Later, they retired to the main dining room where a table had been set aside so they could listen to the solo artist for the evening.

Ryan was on his way to sit down when he ran into a familiar Falling Brook couple, Joshua Lowell and Sophie Armstrong. He'd met Joshua Lowell at his first interview for the CEO position. There was no way to forget him. With his angular face and stone-hewed jaw, the six-foot, broad-shouldered, dark blond with sharp hazel eyes looked more like a model than he did the CEO for an investment firm.

"Ryan?" Joshua was the first to speak.

"Mr. Lowell."

"Joshua, please. I didn't realize you were in town," Joshua said.

"I don't live here. It's Mom's birthday." Ryan glanced behind him to see that his parents were already seated. "We're—" he inclined his head to Jessie at his side "—here to celebrate."

"I'm sorry, I don't believe we've met." Joshua extended his hand to Jessie.

Her eyes narrowed and she didn't accept his hand. "I know who you are, Joshua Lowell."

He frowned. "My reputation. Or shall I say, family's reputation, precedes me."

"It's a small town," Jessie responded.

Ryan glanced at Jessie and her expression was not one of warmth, like it usually was. Did she blame Joshua for what his father had done? It wasn't like her to be unfair. Changing the subject, Ryan opted for happy news. "Congratulations on your engagement." He smiled at Sophie.

Joshua beamed down at the petite reporter whose wavy, highlighted brown hair fell in waves to just below her shoulders. She was in a tailored dress that suited her slim figure. "Thank you," Sophie responded. "I was certainly surprised when he announced to the world we were getting married, but I couldn't be happier."

"That's quite a ring," Jessie commented, and Sophie was eager to show off her diamond ring.

While Sophie gushed about her ring, Joshua whispered, "I want you to know, I was very impressed with your credentials, Ryan. You are very high on our list of a few select candidates. I look forward to our next interview."

Ryan grinned. "Thank you. I appreciate you saying that."

"No, I absolutely mean it," Joshua said. "You have a passion for what you do, more than I ever did. Although I majored in economics in college, art has always been and will always be what wakes me up in the morning."

"Why did you stay so long at Black Crescent?"

"I felt responsible to clean up the mess my father made. To try to make amends as best I could. And I've done that. Or at least, all I can. It's time for me to hand the baton off."

"Are you men talking shop?" Sophie inquired.

Ryan could see the wheels of her journalistic mind churning, thinking up another story.

"C'mon, honey, let's leave these two to their evening," Joshua said. "Ryan…" He shook his hand. "We'll talk soon."

The couple left, but Jessie was still staring at them. "Omigod. *She's* the reporter who wrote the Black Crescent anniversary article."

"One and the same."

"I'm surprised he could forgive her, given he didn't come out smelling like a rose in the story."

Ryan shrugged. "Opposites attract, right?" He and Jessie were certainly at opposite ends of the spectrum when it came to him accepting a job at Black Crescent. He wanted the challenge and she wanted him to forget about it. They were never going to agree, so he held out his hand. "Let's dance." She accepted and took his hand.

On the dance floor, he pulled Jessie into his arms. "I know this is rather public," he said. "You okay?"

She tilted her head to look up at him.

"I've never had a more fantastic night. Your family…" He saw tears in her eyes. "They're amazing. So warm and inviting. They made me feel like I belong. I've never felt that way with my family. I've always felt like I had to put on a show and do what's expected. It's a relief to just be myself."

"That's because you belong with me." And before he knew what he was doing, he was kissing her. He hadn't meant to, but she was looking at him so adoringly and with the songstress crooning "At Last," Ryan forgot where he was.

When he lifted his head, Jessie was staring at him intently. It was a turning point. They'd just announced to everyone in the country club that they were a couple.

Jessie was overcome and immediately excused herself to go to the ladies' room. She hadn't expected Ryan to kiss her like that, out in the open where anyone could see them. But now that he had, didn't she feel a little bit relieved?

They were no longer a secret. And soon everyone in Falling Brook would know. Jessie was under no illusions word wouldn't get around. It was a town of two thousand people and many of them knew the O'Malleys and would no doubt be telling them they'd seen her kissing Ryan Hathaway. Although she and Hugh were on a break, their parents didn't know that.

Once again, Jessie was repairing her lipstick in the mirror when the door to the restroom opened. Ryan's mother entered. "There you are. I was wondering where you'd escaped to."

Jessie laughed nervously. "I needed to use the rest-room."

"Aww, honey, we both know that's not the real reason you're in here. You're running away from what's going on between you and my son."

"I'm not running away."

"I'm not blind, Jessie. You and Ryan used to be so close, the best of friends, but then your father fell on hard times. There were rumors you and your brother received a scholarship from O'Malley Motors. Suddenly, you and that O'Malley boy were thick as thieves and you and Ryan were no more. And I never understood how that could happen because I always felt you and Ryan might grow into more one day. And I was right."

Jessie shook her head. "Mrs. Hathaway, you don't understand…"

"Oh yes, I do." His mother reached for both of Jessie's hands and clasped them in hers. "I understand you've been fighting your own heart for some time and doing what others expect of you because you think you owe them. When are you going to allow yourself to do what *you* want to do? Life is too short, Jessie. You have to grab your happiness when it comes. *With* whomever it comes."

"Thank you, Mrs. Hathaway." She squeezed her hand. "I appreciate your sage advice. And let me say, happy birthday."

"So the cat is out of the bag," Ben said when he and Sean found Ryan outside, interminably pacing the terrace.

"I was wondering how long you were going to be able to resist telling the whole world."

Ryan chuckled. "Whoever knew my brother could be a comedian. I crossed the line out there. I told Jessie we would keep our relationship private until she was ready to go public, and I go and blow it."

Ben came toward him and grasped his shoulder. "Don't be so hard on yourself. You dig the girl. And you wanted to show it. There's nothing wrong with that."

"And the idea of you two staying private was ridiculous," Sean stated, "when it's so obvious by looking at the two of you that you're crazy about each other."

"You're seeing things," Ryan responded. "Jessie doesn't feel that way about me. We're compatible in the bedroom."

"TMI," Ben said. "And we both have two eyes. If we can see it, so can everyone else in that room." He pointed to the ballroom.

Ryan stared through the double doors. Could he believe Jessie was developing feelings for him? He was afraid to think it, let alone believe it. For months, he'd vowed to keep his distance after pining away for years, but now he was getting in deeper than ever.

No, he had to keep his feelings to himself. Act as if he didn't care until Jessie was ready to say those three words.

The return limo drive was a bit more subdued. Jessie didn't mean to be a buzzkill, but she'd listened to what Mrs. Hathaway'd had to say and knew she had a lot of thinking to do.

When they made it to the Hathaway residence, she wished them all good-night and walked in silence with

Ryan the short distance to her parents' front door. She fumbled her keys out of her clutch and dropped them on the front step.

"I've got it." Ryan bent to pick them up. He handed them to her and a fizz of electricity sparked between them. "Jessie, I'm sorry about tonight. If I embarrassed you in any way."

She shook her head. "Well, you did. I thought we agreed to keep our relationship between us? I thought you understood that. Now everyone in Falling Brook will know. Word will get back to my parents, to Hugh."

"Is Hugh all you care about?" She could see he was visibly angry at her mentioning his name.

"I've told you how hard it's been living up to my parents' expectations, and I intended to talk to them in my own time, but you've forced the issue."

"Maybe it needed to be forced, so you can finally make a choice."

Jessie ran her fingers through her hair. "Why do you do this? Why do you always push me?"

"Because if I don't, who will?" he responded hotly. "You'll keep doing as everyone expects instead of being true to you. Wake up, Jessie!"

"I have to go," Jessie said, turning on her heel. "Are you still going to give me a ride back into the city?"

He nodded. "Of course. That hasn't changed. Have fun with your family at Top Golf."

She glared at him. She didn't know how that was going to be possible when word would get back to her parents that she was dallying with Ryan.

Using her key, she opened the front door, stepped inside, closed it and leaned against it.

"Is something going on between you and Ryan Hathaway?" She heard her mother's voice in the darkness.

"Not now, Mama."

"I thought you were with Hugh." Her mother moved out of the shadows. Her arms were folded across her chest, looking as if Jessie had disappointed her. She was in her pajamas, which meant she'd waited up after Jessie told her not to. "I got a call from one of my friends that she saw you and Ryan kissing at the country club."

"I said not now, Mama," Jessie bit out and then rushed up the stairs to the guest bedroom. She wouldn't stand being Twenty Questioned about her love life by her own mother. She had a right to make decisions for herself. To choose whom she wanted to love.

Love.

Was it possible she'd fallen in love with Ryan?

If so, she'd done it unconsciously. She'd assumed their sexual chemistry was why she'd felt so close to him, but perhaps she was wrong. Perhaps Mrs. Hathaway was right and Ryan was who she was supposed to be with all along. But it had taken the reunion to show her that the man of her dreams was right in front of her face the entire time.

Thirteen

Ryan worried Jessie would be upset with him when they drove back to Manhattan, but she wasn't anything other than her usual self. When he'd picked her up, he'd thought he'd glimpsed something resembling a frown on Mrs. Acosta's face. But in an instant it was gone, so Ryan figured everything had gone well. "Did you have a good time at Top Golf?" Ryan asked once they were out of Falling Brook and settled on the interstate.

"We did. Daddy absolutely loved it," Jessie said. "It was the first time I'd seen him animated in a long time."

"That's great."

"Yeah, it was nice to go out as a family and not be about doom and gloom. Today was about the Acostas having a fun day out. We need more of them."

"If there's anything I can do to help, let me know,"

Ryan stated. "The Hathaway clan was very excited to have you share Mom's birthday with us."

"I'm glad I went."

"Are you sure about that?" Ryan asked, glancing in her direction. "We haven't had a chance to really talk about what happened at the country club other than a few minutes last night."

"You mean the kiss you planted on me?" Jessie's cheeks pinked.

"I was completely out of line. All I can tell you is that I got caught up in the moment. Having you in my arms, it seemed like the most natural thing to do."

"But we'd agreed to keep our relationship between us," Jessie responded evenly. "Do you have any idea what you did? My mom cornered me last night, then again at Top Golf about us, wanting to know when we became more than friends. She suggested the kiss was you staking your claim so everyone in Falling Brook knows we're together."

Ryan frowned. That's the last thing he'd been thinking. "That wasn't why I kissed you. How could you think that?"

"When you say one thing and then do the opposite, it does leave me to wonder."

Ryan tensed and his fingers clutched the wheel. He hadn't realized how upset Jessie would be, but he supposed it was naïve on his part to think this would blow over. "So you're okay to be on my arm as a friend, but nothing more. Heaven forbid anyone sees us as anything else and upsets the apple cart."

"Don't put words in my mouth." Jessie mouth firmed

in a straight line. "We'd agreed on this before we left Manhattan and you blatantly went against my wishes."

Ryan glanced in her direction and found her gaze focused on him. "I didn't do it *blatantly*."

Her eyes narrowed as if she didn't believe him.

"How long have you known me? Have I ever given you a reason *not* to trust me, Jessie?"

"No."

"Then don't pick a fight. I said I'm sorry and I am. I would never want to put you in an awkward situation. You know that."

She nodded, folding her arms across her chest.

Ryan wanted to know what she was thinking, but she was closed off and doing a good impression of ignoring him. And he hated it. He wanted her to feel like she could talk to him about anything, like she always had. "Whatever is bothering you, you can talk to me about it."

"I can't." She turned her head and stared out of the window. Jessie wished she could talk to her dearest friend about what she was feeling, but she couldn't. *He* was the reason she was in such turmoil.

She suspected she'd fallen in love with Ryan.

She'd never expected their relationship to take the turn it had and it scared her. She'd only ever been with Hugh and theirs hadn't been a normal relationship. And her parents' certainly wasn't an example. Their lack of affection or passion couldn't be healthy. Jessie didn't know how to do this love thing, which made it difficult to confide in Ryan. If she wasn't sure of how she felt, how could she possibly talk to him?

Her mother already recognized their relationship wasn't what she'd led her to believe. She'd cornered Jessie at Top Golf when they were in the restroom, asking her when their relationship had become romantic, but Jessie had remained mum. Not only was she trying to keep her word to Hugh, but she'd pointed out to her mother that their relationship was none of her business. Her mother hadn't been happy with her answer.

Jessie had never had a close relationship with Angela Acosta. She'd always been a daddy's girl, which was why she'd always wanted to do what her parents asked—to please him. She's supposed that's why it hurt so much to see her father in such pain over what happened fifteen years ago. She wanted him to move on with his life, but he was mired in the past. No matter how well she did as an attorney and gave back to her parents, in her father's mind, it would never be what he once had.

That was why she didn't want Ryan to take the job at Black Crescent. The company's legacy was painful for so many people, her father included. Jessie was certain when the time came, Ryan would do the right thing.

"We're here," Ryan said, turning off the engine and jumping out of the vehicle.

Jessie glanced up and saw that Ryan had parked in front of her brownstone. She hopped out and found him pulling her overnight bag from the trunk. "I've got it."

She tried to take the bag from him, but he glared at her. "I'll walk you up."

They were quiet as they climbed the stairs and Jessie opened the door to her apartment. Ryan deposited her bag in her bedroom and turned to face her. "Whenever you want to talk, I'm a phone call away."

"You're leaving?"

"That's what you want, isn't it? You're clearly still upset with me, so I'm giving you some space."

"Ryan…"

He held up his hands. "It's okay. Take some time, but then call me later."

Jessie heard his footsteps on the hardwood floors and then the door closing on his way out. She wanted to stop Ryan, to tell him to stay, but she didn't. She couldn't when she was so conflicted. And then it hit her: she had some unfinished business to sort out before she could move forward with Ryan.

"Ryan, we can stop at any minute," Dennis, his trainer, said after he'd completed two grueling hours of physical activity.

"It's all right. I can keep going."

"Well, I can't," Dennis said, laughing. "I have another client coming in. I agreed to come in early because you said you needed to burn off some excess energy, but you've done enough for the day."

He tossed Ryan a towel, which he caught. Wiping the sweat from his face, Ryan reached for a Powerade and drank the entire bottle. He'd pushed himself physically as far as he could go because he hadn't wanted to think about Jessie. But it was hopeless. He'd fallen hopelessly, irrevocably, in love with her. He'd known it since the Hamptons, had tried to fight the inevitable, but there it was.

Last night he hadn't been able to sleep because, in the few weeks they'd been together, Ryan had begun to get used to sleeping beside Jessie each night. He loved having her behind curved against his front and his arms wrapped around her slender frame.

Needless to say, he was cranky. But it was a new day and he had much to look forward to. He anticipated hearing from Allison Randall, the recruiter from Black Crescent any day now. He'd interviewed nearly a month ago. She'd told him they were taking their time selecting the right person with a vision on how to move the company forward.

Ryan was no longer sure it was him. He and Jessie were already on thin ice. If he accepted the position, their relationship would be over. He was certain Jessie wouldn't appreciate her boyfriend working for the company that ruined her father. That put Ryan between a rock and a hard place. Go after success, which was in his reach, or choose the woman he loved? If he was chosen, he would be required to make a decision and Ryan hoped he would make the right one.

Ryan was in her head too much. She'd been at work for hours and had missed a court filing for a case one of the senior partners was working on. She'd had to beg the court clerk for an extension, which thankfully had been granted. Otherwise, her boss would have her head on a stick if she hadn't managed to correct her error.

Now she'd been staring at a brief she needed to finish for another partner and had only written a few paragraphs. *What was wrong with her?* Work had always been her respite. Her refuge from the storm. She'd never had a problem focusing, but then again, she'd never had Ryan Hathaway as a lover.

Whenever she was around him, any idea or thought she had flew right out the window. But she hadn't seen him last night. In an effort to gain some perspective, she'd spent the evening apart from him, though her body was revolting in protest. She literally ached to be with him. To see his handsome face light up when she walked into a room. To hear him laugh at one of her corny knock-knock jokes. To feel him buried so deep inside her she didn't know where she left off and he began. To taste the spiciness of his cologne on his brown skin.

Jessie wanted all of it, but on the other hand, she felt as if she was on a dangerous precipice and if she fell the wrong way, she'd fall headlong into disaster. One road led her on the path her parents envisioned for her with Hugh. The other less-known road led her to Ryan, who was always pushing her to live her life on her own terms. But Jessie was afraid of taking the road less traveled. If she revealed her feelings—that she was falling for Ryan—and their relationship didn't materialize into more, she would have ruined the greatest friendship of her life.

And what did more mean? Marriage? Babies? For years, all she'd had to keep her warm at night was her dedication and focus on her career. On achieving success, so she would never end up like her father. She'd been on the well-known, expected path for years and was on her way to making junior partner. But the victory had begun to seem hollow with no one to share it with. She'd thought that person was Hugh, but over the years had realized it didn't feel the same.

He was the upstanding guy everyone thought he was, and their relationship had always been one of mutual respect, but he didn't make her heart skip a beat or make her ache for him. The times they'd been intimate had been perfunctory and certainly lacking the passion she shared with Ryan. It only took one searing look from Ryan to make her panties damp. Or a drugging kiss like the one he'd given her at the country club for her to lose all thought as to where they were.

Ryan was in her blood. She was weak and defenseless when it came to him. The last few weeks certainly made Jessie believe they could have more, but she was afraid to take the leap. Look at her judgment when it came to Hugh. She'd allowed the relationship to go on much longer than she should have. She should have ended it years ago, but she'd used him as a crutch to keep Ryan at arm's length.

But she did owe Hugh the respect of having a heart-to-heart conversation and finally tell him there was no hope of resurrecting their relationship—so she could have a future. A future that may include Ryan.

Ryan knew he should give Jessie the space she asked for, but it had been over forty-eight hours since the kiss at the country club. Surely, Jessie had calmed down by now? That's what he told himself as he waited outside her apartment door.

Becca answered, fully dressed, her hair done up and her makeup flawless. "Hey, Ryan. C'mon in. I was just leaving for a date, but Jessie's in there." She inclined her head down the hall to Jessie's bedroom. Then she flew out the front door.

Ryan took the pizza box and six-pack of beer he'd brought with him and placed it on the counter. He was looking through the cupboard for some paper plates when Jessie came padding through the kitchen in a tank top, running shorts and her favorite pair of fuzzy bunny slippers. Her face had been wiped clean of makeup, but was bright and clear. Her eyes, however, grew wide when they saw him. "I thought I heard the door, but assumed it was Becca leaving."

"Yeah, I kind of caught her on the way out." Ryan paused from shuffling through her cabinets and pulled a bottle of beer from the carton. He unscrewed it and handed it to Jessie.

"Thanks," She tipped it back and took a swig. She wiped her mouth with the back of her hand. "What are you doing here?"

"I brought dinner." He pointed to the pizza box. "I hope you don't mind? I have cheese and pineapple."

That he still remembered her favorite pizza brought a smile to her face and he released a sigh of relief. Showing up unannounced was a gamble, but he had to do something. They couldn't go on like this.

"Thanks. I am kind of hungry. I skipped lunch." She opened the pizza box without getting a plate and began eating.

"Why?"

"Struggled writing this brief for the senior partner and it was due by six. I think he purposely gives me these deadlines to screw with me." She finished the slice in record time.

"Did you finish?"

"Barely." She swigged her beer. "Today was not my best day."

"Because you're still angry with me?" Ryan surmised.

Jessie shook her head. "I'm not angry. Not anymore."

Ryan brushed a hand across his forehead. "Thank God. I hope you know I got carried away. It's no excuse for not keeping my word. And I'm sorry."

"I believe you," Jessie said. "I always did. The problem isn't *us*. It's that no one knows Hugh and I broke up."

Ryan frowned. "I don't understand."

"We discussed going our separate ways in private, but hadn't quite had the nerve to tell our families and friends."

Ryan digested this information. "So anyone who was there Saturday night thinks you're cheating on Hugh with me?"

Jessie nodded. "But I don't care about any of that. Or what people think about me. I stopped caring a long time ago after my family and I were ostracized when we lost everything. I worry about my parents and what they think and how they feel. You know my father hasn't been in a good way for years. This could derail him. He's been depending on me to do what's expected and I feel bad because I told Hugh we would tell everyone when the time was right."

"The *time* is right," Ryan stated. He didn't understand what the holdup was. Or perhaps he'd been fooling himself. He thought back to the conversation he'd had with Jessie on the deck of the Hampton beach house. She had said they were on a break and he'd gotten it in his mind that it was a breakup. That's certainly what Jessie had led him to believe. But maybe she was holding out hope that, with time apart, Hugh would see the error of his ways and come crawling back. *Was this all part of some elaborate power play to get him to heel? To get Hugh to finally put a ring on it and stop procrastinating?*

"It's going to have to be," Jessie said. "I left him a message last night that we needed to talk."

"I see."

She eyed him suspiciously. "What's wrong?"

Everything. He'd gotten in too deep with Jessie, even though he'd vowed not to, and she was walking away, doing what her family expected by choosing Hugh. It was beginning to appear that Ryan had been the fool to believe it was truly over between Jessie and Hugh and he finally had a chance of winning her heart when the deck was stacked against him. His phone vibrated in his pocket. He saw the display with the caller's name and knew what he had to do. It was time he finally pursued what was best for him. He couldn't let Jessie or her reaction influence his decision.

Swiping left, he answered.

"Ryan. Hi, it's Allison Randall."

Ryan glanced down at his watch. It was rather late

for her to call, but he was happy nonetheless. "Hi, Allison. It's good to hear from you."

"I apologize for the late hour, but I wanted you to know how impressed we were with you and we would like to bring you back for a second interview so you can talk with Joshua about your specific ideas for replacing him as CEO."

"Did Joshua tell you I ran into him in Falling Brook?"

"Yes, he did," Allison replied. "Which is why he told me not to waste any more time. You made a great first impression."

"Thank you, Allison. When would he like to meet?"

"I'll email you a couple of date/time options."

"That would be great. I'll clear my schedule."

"Wonderful," Allison responded. "We'll talk soon. Take care."

"You do the same." Ryan ended the call and, when he did, the somber expression on Jessie's face told him she was not happy about his decision to move forward with the interview process.

"I thought you had forgotten about Black Crescent," Jessie said, placing her beer bottle on the counter.

"Why would you think that?"

Jessie glared. "I don't know." She shrugged. "Maybe because we discussed how taking this position would be an awful idea. Not just for you, but for me and my family. Heck, the entire community. Black Crescent needs to fail so we all can move on with our lives."

"I understand your position, Jessie. But it's not your decision to make. It's mine. Whether I do or do not pursue Black Crescent is my choice. I don't appreciate you trying to dictate my future."

"That's not what I'm doing."

"Aren't you?" he inquired. "Would you be making this same request of me if we weren't sleeping together?"

"How dare you?" She huffed, pushing away from the counter. "One thing has nothing to do with the other. It's a bad move. And I would think, after everything that's happened, everything you witnessed me and my family go through, you would be more sympathetic. But clearly I was wrong. You can only see what *you* want and forget about everyone else."

"Christ! I really can't believe you, of all people, would say that to me," Ryan replied. "I've always been there for you, Jessie. Always been an ear to listen or a shoulder to cry on. Look up the word 'empathetic' and you'll find my picture. It's you who's being unfair."

"Me?"

"If the shoe fits," he returned. "I would never ask you to give up on your dreams. Instead, all I've ever done is champion your goals. Yet that's what you're asking me to do—to give up something I feel strongly about. When you won't compromise yourself. You're not willing to go after the life you want, to break away from your family, but I am, especially if I can't have you."

Jessie's phone rang and she stalked away from him and pulled it out of her purse. "Hello?"

Ryan couldn't hear anything because she turned her back to him. His antenna went up. "Who's on the phone, Jessie?" He stormed toward her.

She held up a finger, telling Ryan to give her a minute, and stepped away to talk in her bedroom. "I'm sorry now isn't a good time to talk, Hugh."

So Hugh was on the line?

Was it fate that the man who was standing between them would call when they were in the middle of their fight? Ryan didn't like that Jessie had turned her back and tried to hide it from him, not wanting him to hear their conversation. If nothing else, he thought they had trust between them. He was wrong which meant they no longer had a future—Jessie wasn't willing to take a risk, to defy her parents and to choose him.

Hugh's timing was the epitome of bad. Why did he have to call her now? She and Ryan had never fought like this before, but this was big. He wanted Jessie to break away from her family, but she couldn't do that. So their entire relationship was at stake and not just their romance. If he took that job with Black Crescent, it would end their friendship, as well.

"Are you listening to me, Jessie?" Hugh asked on the other end of the line.

"I'm sorry, what did you say?"

"Did I catch you at a bad time?"

"Yeah, kind of…sort of." Jessie didn't want to give away that she was with another man. Hugh had never taken kindly to her friendship with Ryan. He'd never forbidden their association, but he'd been uneasy of Jessie's openness with Ryan.

"All right, well, I wanted you to know that I'm coming home to Falling Brook."

"You are?"

"Yes, these last several months apart have really made me see some things differently and I'd like to talk to you in person about some realizations I've had after I did some serious soul-searching."

"Hugh, I don't think that's going to change anything." She had to end things with him once and for all. There was no going back, not after the last month she'd spent with Ryan. It was time Jessie found her own way. She needed to stop doing what Hugh or her parents wanted. She needed to do what she wanted. She and Hugh had a superficial, surface-level relationship at best. They would never truly make one another happy.

"C'mon, Jessie. After everything we've been to each other, don't I at least deserve that much?"

Guilt ate at Jessie's insides. He was right. She owed him enough to let him speak his piece. "Of course. When are you coming in?"

"End of the week."

"All right, I'll see you then."

"And, Jessie…"

"Yes?"

"I miss you." He ended the call, not waiting for her response. And thank goodness he hadn't because she didn't feel the same. She'd hardly given Hugh a thought unless she was comparing how different he and Ryan were.

She returned to the living room and found Ryan with his back to her. She didn't need to be a genius to notice the tension in the set of his shoulders. He was angry. Not just about her stance on his taking the Black Crescent position, but about her call with Hugh.

"Ryan."

He didn't move. Instead, he faced forward, staring out her window as if it had all the answers. "Are you running back to Hugh now because you and I are having a disagreement? Is that what this is?"

Jessie fumed. "Of course not. Why would you think that? Because I took a call?"

He spun around to face her and the dejected look on his face broke her heart. She hated that she was the cause of Ryan's distress. "It's me, Jessie. The man who has been by your side for over half your life listening to you fawn over Hugh O'Malley."

"And you've always been angry about that."

"Yes!"

"You don't like Hugh."

"No, I don't."

"And you resent our relationship?"

"Yes!"

She stared at him and finally saw the truth. "How long have you felt this way?"

"Are you blind, Jessie? I've always wanted you," Ryan stated. "But you never saw me—" when she started to speak, he cut her off, shaking his head "—not until the reunion when we had a moment on the terrace. That's when you recognized the attraction between us. But as soon as Hugh showed up, you walked away. That's when I knew I should move on. But now I've been with you, I want you to stay, but you have to want it, too."

"Don't do that. Don't you make me out to be the bad guy."

"I'm not. I'm stating *I'm* the man for you, Jessie. I always have been and I always will be."

Ryan stared at her expectantly and Jessie's breath caught in her throat. She'd never been as honest and forthright with her feelings as Ryan was being now. He was laying it all on the line, baring his soul to her. And what could she do? She hadn't sorted out all of her feelings yet.

He sucked in a harsh breath. "I guess I'm completely alone in my feelings and clearly misguided." He started toward the door.

"Ryan, wait."

"Why? You don't know what you want. And if you do, it isn't me. It's Hugh."

"Stop putting words in my mouth. You have no idea what's going on here. I…" Jessie didn't know how to verbalize the thoughts rumbling around in her head. How she didn't know how to escape the confines of following her parents' expectations that were so ingrained her. That she'd only just begun to find herself the last few weeks, but was afraid of taking the leap. Hugh and Ryan deserved so much better than she was giving either of them at the moment.

"Yes, I do. You're never going to choose me," Ryan responded quietly. "So that's my cue to leave." His footsteps were sure and strong, and when he reached her front door, he turned to her. She wanted to tell him to stay. She wanted him to wrap his arms around her and tell her everything was going to be okay and they would work through this. But he didn't. He merely opened the door and walked out.

Jessie feared he was walking out of her life for good. And she couldn't bear that. Rushing to the window, she caught sight of him jumping into his Porsche and speeding off into the night. Had she done the right thing letting him walk away? Or had she just made the biggest mistake of her life?

Fourteen

"Jessie!" Hugh picked her up off her feet and wrapped her in a hug the moment she stepped foot in the guest-house at the O'Malley residence on Friday evening. She'd come straight from work, taken the train and then an Uber from the station. The journey had been tumultuous and not because of the ride. Jessie had been thinking about Ryan and how angry he'd been with her. She'd needed his understanding while she figured out what to do next, but patience wasn't Ryan's virtue. Instead, he kept pressing her to decide, decide, decide. She would in her own time. And she had. On the train ride, Jessie had known she needed to end things with Hugh. They couldn't go on in limbo, not when she was in love with bullheaded, sexy Ryan. Why wasn't life easy?

"Hugh—" she patted his shoulders while peering into his brilliant sky-blue eyes "—put me down."

He laughed and did as she asked, but didn't let go of her. Instead, he kept his arm circled around her waist. "It's so good to see you, babe."

"You're looking well." Jessie politely removed his hand and moved further into the house. "How does it feel to be back in the States?"

Hugh's handsome features had grown sharper and more defined since the last time she'd seen him. He was clean-shaved and didn't have rugged stubble like Ryan. His dark hair was expertly cut, stopping just above the collar of his tailored three-piece charcoal suit with its frosted-gray tie.

"Better now that you're here," Hugh said, following her into the living room. The room was immaculately decorated in soft creams and pastels with furniture Jessie knew was custom made. An Impressionist painting hung on the wall, showing how well off his family truly was. "Come sit beside me." He patted the empty spot on the sofa.

It seemed rude to resist, so reluctantly she sat beside him, but on the far side of the couch.

"I don't bite, Jessie. Or at least not unless you want me," he chuckled. When she didn't smile, he frowned. "Surely, we haven't been apart so long we can't joke with one another?"

"We've been apart for our *entire* relationship, Hugh. What do you expect?"

"Ouch." His eyes darkened as he held her gaze. "I guess I deserve that, but that's why I'm here. I've recognized I've put our relationship on the back burner and focused too much on my career."

"Yes, you have," Jessie said, running her fingers through her straight hair, "but I can't put it all on you. I never said anything or required more of you. I've been content to be put aside because I always thought one day we would find our way back to each other."

"But you don't feel that way now?"

Jessie shook her head and he placed his hand over his heart.

"I'm sorry. I'm not saying this to hurt you, Hugh, but when I look back, we haven't been in the same city since we were in prep school. That's no way to start the foundation for a relationship, much less a marriage."

"I know that, Jessie. Truly I do. It's why I'm here. I'm glad you told me we needed to take a break and figure out what it is we really want. Because it made me see that it's you I want. It's always been you, but I've been too blinded by my own ambition and lost sight of what's really important. But I'm ready now. I'm willing to find a job in Manhattan so we can work on our relationship. I've already sent my résumé to some executive recruitment specialists and put out some feelers."

"That's great, Hugh, but I've thought about it and I don't want you to move here. You don't really want to, and you're only doing it because you think it's what you *should* do. You should come back because you *want* to."

"I do want to," he stated more firmly.

"Are you trying to convince me or yourself?" Jessie inquired.

"What's gotten into you?" Hugh asked, hopping to

his feet. He began pacing the marble floor and then spun around to stare at her. "You've never spoken to me like this before."

"We need to be honest with ourselves about what it is we truly want, Hugh. Do you really want to be with me? Or are you with me because it's the right thing to do? Or what your parents expect of you? Are you even in love with me?" Jessie knew she didn't have those feelings for him. "So much so, you can't see your life without me? That's the kind of love I'm talking about. That's the kind of love I want."

"I don't think now is the right time to talk to you," Hugh said, shaking his head. "Clearly you're not in the right headspace to have such a serious conversation about our future."

"What do you expect our marriage to look like?" Jessie persisted. She wasn't dropping this conversation. "A white picket fence? Two kids? Live in Falling Brook or Connecticut and have the perfect life?"

"Yeah, Jess. Maybe that is what I want," Hugh snapped back. "Is something so wrong with that? Because, correct me if I'm wrong, but I thought that's what you wanted too. What you and I have been working our butts off to achieve?"

Hugh had a point. That's what she'd *thought* she wanted.

The O'Malleys had done so much for her during her youth. If it hadn't been for the scholarship Jack O'Malley had given her and Pete, she would have never gotten into a good university. And Hugh...well, he'd always been a constant. The good-looking, popular boy every girl in Falling Brook had wanted, including her. She'd thought herself lucky he'd given her the time of day. But as the years had gone by, she'd become increasingly dissatisfied with her life, and Hugh hadn't been around to see that.

"Dreams change, Hugh. And maybe, if you'd been around, you'd know that. I no longer want this perfect life where we are slaves to our careers and making money. Not to say there's anything wrong with being ambitious and striving for success. I've learned that love and passion are equally as important."

She didn't love him and never would. She loved Ryan. And she may have lost him because she was too afraid to take a chance, but she wouldn't compound the mistake by making another.

It was time she took control of her life. She'd lived too long under the shadow of her parents' expectations. She was taking the first step, ending it with Hugh because she was in love with another man.

Ryan.

"You've found love and passion with someone else, haven't you?"

A tear slid down Jessie's cheek. "I have. And you deserve someone who can love you with her whole heart and without reservation. And I'm not that woman."

Hugh lowered his head and Jessie felt terrible for hurting him, but it couldn't be helped. They could no longer go on like this, not when her heart belonged to someone else.

When Hugh finally lifted his head, Jessie was surprised to see unshed tears in his blue eyes. "I understand it's for the best. I should never have taken you for granted, assumed you would be there when I finally got my act together."

Jessie gave a half smile. "I didn't try hard enough, either." Because she'd been unhappy and restless for years. "Anyway, we're going to need to tell our families that we're no longer together. I know it'll be tough on your family, but I hope they know how grateful I am for everything they've done."

Hugh frowned in exasperation. "You never owed us anything, Jessie. I hope you know that."

She hadn't, but she did now. "I do. I do now."

"Can I ask who it is—the man you're in love with? Or do I already know?" Hugh inquired.

"What do you mean?"

"It's Ryan. Isn't it?"

Jessie wanted to end their relationship with a clear conscience. She was done with the lies. She owed Hugh the truth. "Yes."

Hugh shook his head and a wry laugh escaped his lips. "I guess I should have known. I'm surprised he waited this long to make a play for you."

"It wasn't like that…we just sort of happened."

"Jessie, Jessie, Jessie." Hugh released an exasperated breath. "Open your eyes, it's always been Ryan. He's loved you from afar for years. Even I saw it. I've always been jealous of the friendship and easy camaraderie you two shared."

Jessie frowned. "You were? I never knew."

"I hid it well underneath bravado because I thought I was the best man for you. I can see I was wrong." He leaned in for a hug. "I wish you all the best, Jess. I truly do. All I've ever wanted is your happiness."

Jessie reached out and stroked his cheek. "I want the same for you, Hugh. And one day you will find the person that completes you, like I have."

Hugh offered a wry smile and inclined his head to the door. "Go on. Get out of here. Go get your man."

Jessie grinned. "I intend to do just that, I just have to wrap up some family business first." She gave Hugh one final squeeze and quickly rushed out into the night.

Professionally speaking, Ryan's life was soaring. He'd had a great interview with a Manhattan investment firm that was looking for new leadership since their founding member was retiring. The meeting had gone well and Ryan felt confident he would be called back. Black Crescent wasn't the only show in town.

But they hadn't forgotten about him, either. Joshua Lowell wanted to meet him for a second interview. The former CEO appreciated Ryan's résumé as well his ideas for Black Crescent's future. Allison had called to confirm a Monday meeting in Falling Brook. However, he would be remiss if he didn't admit his thoughts had strayed to Jessie during the call with Allison.

What would she think about him going through with the interview? He knew she was adamantly opposed to his working for the enemy after the pain the firm had caused her family, but Ryan strongly believed he could make a difference.

Quite frankly, he wasn't sure there was a relationship to fight for because she couldn't break away from her parents. Ryan wanted all or nothing. He hadn't heard from Jessie the last several days and it was driving him crazy. No amount of late hours at the office or working out with Dennis was going to ease the tension he felt. He wanted to call her, but what would he say that he hadn't said earlier in the week?

He'd bared his soul to her. Shared how much he cared for her, and she'd stared back at him with her doe eyes and hadn't said a word. What was he supposed to think, let alone feel about her silence? Was she afraid to tell him "thank you for the orgasms and take a hike"?

Ryan was desperate to get away from it all and decided to go to Connecticut for the weekend to visit his brother, Ben. He certainly wasn't going to Falling Brook early so his parents could hound him about Jessie. They'd already inquired about her and wondered if she might be the newest addition to the family. Ryan hadn't had the heart to tell them that they couldn't be further off track. Jessie would much prefer to be with the O'Malleys.

Instead, he would spend some quality time with his brother to see if he couldn't put Jessie Acosta in his rearview.

"Hey, baby bro. Come on in." Ben greeted him with a hug when Ryan rang the doorbell later that evening. He'd driven through Friday rush hour to the stunning mountaintop city of Bethel and was treated to some breathtaking views on his way, but now Ryan was ready for a drink.

"Thanks, man," Ryan said, stepping inside the contemporary three-bedroom town house. "Where's the missus?" He'd never been to his brother's new place and appreciated the open floor plan and well-equipped gourmet kitchen with its large center island and plenty of counter space.

"No offense, but you don't come to Connecticut often. She figured we might want some male bonding time, so she's hanging out with her girls tonight. So take a load off." Ben motioned to the leather sectional in the spacious family room Ryan had followed him into. "Can I get you anything? Beer? Wine?"

Ryan's face pinched. "You got something stronger?"

"I've got a nice Scotch if you're interested?"

"Yeah, I'll have that."

"On the rocks?"

Ryan shook his head. "Neat." He relaxed his head against the sofa and tried to let the week's events roll off him, but it wasn't working.

"Looks like you need this." Ryan heard Ben's voice behind him and turned to find his brother extending him a glass of brown liquid.

"I do." Ryan downed the two thumbs. "Another please." He handed the glass back.

"Uh, are you looking to tie one on?" Ben asked.

"Maybe." Ryan rolled his shoulders, but the tension wouldn't leave him. "It's been one crazy week."

Ben joined him on the couch after he'd refilled his glass and brought along the entire bottle of Scotch. "Thought you might need this." He set the bottle down on the coffee table. "So, fill me in. What's been going on? Last I saw you, you and Jessie were hugged up pretty tight on the dance floor."

"And if you recall, she wasn't too happy about that."

"But she's happy to be more than friends when no one's looking. Is that what's got you so riled up?"

"That and then some," Ryan replied, sipping his Scotch. "I learned Jessie didn't exactly break up with Hugh, not officially anyway. So, in essence, it was more of a break than calling it quits. I think she did it to keep up with the expectations her family had for her and O'Malley. She led me to believe we actually had a chance when she was merely biding her time until O'Malley got his act together."

"Do you really think that's true?" Ben inquired, staring at him intently. "As long as I've known Jessie, she's been a good kid." At Ryan's scowl, he amended, "A good woman. I can't imagine she would string you along."

"Well, what am I supposed to think?" Ryan inquired.

"Wait. Be patient."

"I'm done waiting," Ryan said. "Hell, I've waited for her for nearly two decades, but it eats me up because I know she's probably not alone."

"What do you mean?"

"Hugh called her during our argument earlier this week. And since then, I haven't heard a peep from her."

"And you think he's the reason why?"

"Partly. It's also her parents' expectations and her obligations to the O'Malleys," Ryan said, throwing up his hands and rushing to his feet. "I've been competing against him my whole life. And right when I thought it was a fair fight, I find out my hands have been tied behind my back the entire time and she was never really *free* to be with me."

"Ryan, you need to settle down. You're making a lot of assumptions without talking to Jessie."

Ryan didn't think so. Her silence spoke volumes. She wanted nothing more to do with him. It had been fun while it lasted, but now that Hugh had come calling, she was running back to the familiar. When Ryan knew for a fact her physical relationship with Hugh didn't hold a candle to theirs.

He plopped down on the sofa. "As much as it pains me, I can't sit around waiting for Jessie to decide she wants to be with me."

"What are you going to do?"

"Move on, as I'd intended to do before taking her to the Hamptons."

"Can you do that?" Ben asked, watching him intently. "This woman has been an important part of your life. Are you sure you can just cut her off, cold turkey?"

"You act like I'm an addict or something."

Ben chuckled. "I wouldn't go that far, but you have been hooked on her to the detriment of some of your other relationships."

Ryan supposed his brother was right, because none of those other women had ever measured up to Jessie. Whenever his previous relationships started to get serious, he would withdraw. He'd told himself it was because he wasn't ready to commit, but that wasn't the truth. Maybe, deep down, he'd been holding out hope one day Jessie would come around and see him as her Prince Charming. What a fool he'd been.

"You're right," Ryan said. "I have to break the cycle and I will, but I have to talk to Jessie. I need her to tell me to my face that this entire month has been a lie. That it's been nothing more than a summer fling. Only then can I move on."

"I agree. Now, can we please stop bemoaning your woes and watch some baseball? The Yankees are playing tonight and I'd much rather watch them than you cry."

Ryan chuckled. "Sounds like a plan."

"I'm so happy you're home again," Jessie's mother said as they walked through the farmers' market in downtown Falling Brook, perusing vegetables. "I hear Hugh is also back in town."

As if on cue, Kathleen O'Malley appeared from one of the stalls, carrying a basket of fruit. She stopped when she saw Jessie and her mother standing nearby, selecting tomatoes.

"Jessie! It's so fabulous to see you. Hugh told us you were in town."

"Mrs. O'Malley, a pleasure." Jessie air-kissed the woman and inclined her head sideways. "You remember my mother?"

The brunette smile. "I do." Her eyes narrowed as she surveyed her mother for several beats. Jessie wondered why Hugh's mother was giving her such a close inspection. Had the two women had a quarrel?

"It's good to see you…" Jessie said and began to

turn away. "If you'll excuse us?" She was eager to get away from the negative vibes emanating between the two women.

"I was hoping you might join us for dinner tonight?" Mrs. O'Malley's invitation dangled in the air. "We'd love to have you."

Jessie inhaled deeply. Hugh hadn't told his parents about the breakup and neither had she. She was working up to it. "Of course." Jessie offered a smile. She would attend the dinner for old times' sake. She would have to text Hugh later to give him a heads-up.

Fifteen

"Mrs. O'Malley, dinner was delicious," Jessie told the older woman she'd come to admire. Kathleen O'Malley was the epitome of class. She wore a sleeveless floral sheath that flared out at the hips matched with a pair of stylish pumps. Her dark brown hair was swept up in a sophisticated chignon while her makeup and jewelry were subtle yet noticeable.

"Thank you, dear," she responded. "I'm so happy Hugh came home. It was in the nick of time, don't you think?" she whispered as she led Jessie to the sunroom.

"Pardon?" Jessie asked, looking up.

"I was disappointed to hear about your dalliance with the Hathaway young man." Her eyes glinted when she spoke and there was no mistaking that mama bear was out in full effect.

"I didn't tell him," his mother whispered conspiratorially. "He's back now and I believe ready to do right by you. So we'll keep this between us and never speak of it again." She glanced down at Jessie, who could only nod her agreement.

By the time they arrived at the terrace where Mrs. O'Malley had tea and mini-desserts waiting, Jessie had lost her appetite. The lies and deception had to come to an end. She was ready for both of them to come clean with their parents.

"You can come visit us anytime, Jessie," Jack O'Malley stated as he and Hugh joined them. "No need to wait for this one—" he pointed to his only son "—to make an appearance."

"I appreciate that, thank you," Jessie said, sucking in a breath. She was doing her best to be cordial, but she felt like she couldn't breathe. She felt like the walls were caving in all around her and this lunch with Hugh's parents had done little to alleviate her anxiety.

"I hope your visit means you're finally getting serious about your future?" Jack questioned, his piercing gray eyes finding his son's as he waited for a response.

Hugh smiled good-naturedly. "No need to be so heavy-handed, Dad. If you must know, there are big changes, starting with… Jessie and I broke up."

His father roared. "You did what?"

"Hugh!" Jessie rose. "A word, please."

He lifted his shoulders in a shrug. "It's okay, Jessie. I appreciate you keeping up with this charade, but I've got this. Go find your happily-ever-after."

Jessie looked into Hugh's baby blues for the last time

and smiled. "Thank you." She inclined her head to his parents. "And thank you both for everything. I'll never forget it."

It was time she took a page from Hugh's book and was honest with her parents. When she made it to her rental car, she quickly started the engine and sped away.

Jessie found herself pulling into her parents' driveway fifteen minutes later. She noticed her father's car wasn't there and she was thankful. She could start first with her mother and smooth the waters before talking to her father. She was such a daddy's girl and would hate to disappoint him, but she had to live her own life. Dragging herself from the car, Jessie used her key for the front door. "Mama?"

Her mother came in from the kitchen, wiping her apron. "I was making some *ropa vieja* for your father for supper. I'm surprised to see you. I didn't expect you until much later this evening."

"Oh, Mama, where do I begin?" Jessie released a long sigh.

"Honey, what is it?" Her mother circled her arms around Jessie's shoulders and helped her to the couch. "Whatever it is, you can tell me. Surely, we can figure it out."

Jessie shook her head. "Nothing has to be figured out, Mama. It's as simple as this. I'm not marrying Hugh because I'm in love with Ryan," Jessie blurted the words out. As soon as she'd said them, she felt as if she'd been set free. She hadn't realized that trying to deny her feelings was making her heartsick.

"Ryan?" The stricken expression on her mother's face told Jessie she'd shocked her.

Jessie nodded.

"But I thought you said you were just friends."

"We were. I mean, we are. Or then again, maybe not, because I've royally screwed this up. I was so conflicted about wanting to do what's right. What's expected…"

"Darling, you're talking in circles. Why don't you take it from the top and tell me what's going on?"

Jessie took a deep breath and gathered herself together. "Hugh and I… I know it's what you wanted and I did, too, but not anymore."

"I thought he was coming home now to repair your relationship."

"Yes, that's why he's here," she cried, "but it's too late."

"Why? Can you explain?"

"Four months ago, at the prep school reunion, something changed. I don't know why, but it did. Suddenly, Ryan wasn't just my friend. He was a good-looking man who looked at me like he wanted me. But then Hugh surprised me by showing up. When I realized I was having feelings for Ryan, I knew Hugh and I couldn't possibly continue seeing each other. Hugh and I agreed to a break because he understood distance hadn't made our hearts grow fonder."

"So you broke up then, not now?"

Jessie nodded. "Four months ago, we decided to take a break and we chose to keep it private. Tonight we ended it officially."

"Why didn't you say something?" her mother inquired. "I wouldn't have pushed you so much if I'd known your relationship status."

Jessie shrugged. "You didn't do anything wrong, Mama. I did. I thought I'd imagined the attraction I felt for Ryan because he was the boy I grew up with next door, so it couldn't possibly be real. I suppressed my feelings for him for three months until the July Fourth weekend. That's when our relationship changed and we became *more than* friends."

"I see."

"Ryan and I have been seeing each other the last month. And it's been wonderful, Mama. Honestly, it's been the best month of my life. But I struggled with my decision because it wasn't right for our family."

"What do you mean breaking up with Hugh isn't the right thing for us?"

"Because I owe them. We all do. Everything Mr. O'Malley has done for me, for Pete. Because of him, we were allowed to continue at Falling Brook Prep. Keep the house."

The horrified look on her mother's face startled Jessie. "You owe the O'Malleys nothing. You've already paid enough. Your brother working at the dealership during school breaks. And you? You've been devoted to the family, to Hugh, for years. But that doesn't mean you owe them your whole life. Your happiness."

"Oh, Mama." Tears of joy sprang to Jessie's eyes at her mother's words.

"Jack didn't give us the money out of the goodness of his heart."

"Why else would he give us that kind of money?"

Her mother lowered her head. "It's complicated, Jessie." She glanced at Jessie and her expression was haunted.

"Mama?"

"Jack and I have been having an affair for years."

"What do you mean? I don't understand." Jessie didn't want to believe the words coming out of her mother's mouth.

"I'm saying I've been lonely. Losing all his money made your father depressed and withdrawn. You've seen it. Think about it. If you feel that way as his child, imagine how I feel as his wife. I was distraught. I didn't know what I was going to do, how I was going to keep our family together. We were going to lose everything. The house. The cars."

"So that justified you having an affair?"

"No. No, it didn't." Her mother shook her head. "And I never meant it to go that far, but Jack was kind and he listened and one thing led to another, just like it did for you and Ryan."

"It's not the same! You're *married*. Ryan and I are single. How could you do this?" Jessie's head fell into her hands and she cried softly.

"I don't know," her mother said tearfully. "Jack was offering support at a time when I needed it most. I didn't mean for it to happen, but once it did, I didn't know how to stop."

"You should have never started in the first place! But thank God you realized it was wrong."

Her mother looked away and Jessie stared at her in disbelief. "Mama." She grabbed her by the arm. "Please tell me this affair with Mr. O'Malley stopped? Please tell me you came to your senses and realized what you were doing was wrong?"

Angela Acosta shook her head and Jessie clasped her hand over her mouth in horror. "You're still seeing him?"

"We never stopped. I tried, but Jack wouldn't let me go."

"What do you mean he wouldn't let you go? He's married. You're *both* married." Maybe.

"I know how this must sound but, like you, I felt beholden to him because he helped me out by giving me a job at his company and paying me an exorbitant salary, which helped us keep this house. Then he offered to pay for your and Pete's education if we stayed together, and I wanted the very best for you both and I saw it as a win-win. I know it is cliché. Lonely married woman has an affair, but I guess I enjoyed the attention Jack bestowed on me because your father hasn't been interested in me in years."

"That doesn't give you a license to cheat."

Her mother was quiet at the reprimand and Jessie fell into silence. She couldn't believe her mother had been having an affair—at a minimum, fifteen years—with Jack O'Malley. Half her life. It had all been a lie.

"Does Daddy know?"

Angela Acosta shook her head.

"Kathleen O'Malley must know. I saw how she looked at you today."

"Then she must turn a blind eye because she's happy

with the life and privileges she has being Mrs. Jack O'Malley."

"This would kill Daddy if he found out. He looks at Mr. O'Malley as his best friend, all the while he's been cavorting with his wife behind his back."

"I did what I had to do to ensure you and your brother's future wasn't limited by the losses your father suffered at the hand of Black Crescent. You know as well as I do, your father was never the same after he lost his fortune. And when he lost his job a few years after, he had a hard time finding another one. We would have lost the house if Jack hadn't intervened."

"All right, say for instance I believe the pile of hogwash you're giving me. Pete graduated years ago and I've been out of college for six years. Law school has been on my own nickel and I have the student loans to prove it. So why are you still with Jack O'Malley?"

Her mother shrugged and Jessie could see she didn't have a pat answer. "Convenience? Companionship? Familiarity? What? Why have you continued this affair after your kids were gone?"

"Because I didn't want to be alone!" her mother yelled passionately, meeting Jessie's eyes without flinching. "If I stayed here with your father, without any companionship or affection, I would shrivel up and die."

"Finally, we're being honest with one another," Jessie retorted with cold sarcasm. "But if you're so unhappy, why don't you divorce Daddy?"

"If I did that, it would break him," her mother responded. "It would be the final nail in his coffin of failures. Do you believe your father could withstand the blow? Because I don't think so."

She was right. Jessie doubted her father could take knowing his best friend and his wife were together. It would kill him. Of that, Jessie was sure.

"My whole point in telling you all of this was that I don't want you to feel obliged to the O'Malleys. You owe them nothing."

"What if there are repercussions from breaking things off with Hugh? We told his parents tonight. Will Mr. O'Malley retaliate and tell Dad the truth?"

Her mother shook her head. "Jack would never do that, not if he wants to continue having a relationship with me. He would never hurt me that way. Plus, it would ruin his marriage."

Jessie's eyes grew large. "You're going to continue seeing him, aren't you?"

"I care for him a great deal," her mother said. "It's not that simple."

"And Daddy?"

"I care for your father and love him in my own way, and you're just going to have to accept that answer."

Jessie glared at her mother. She didn't know what to make of any of this, but knew she wouldn't be like her mother, staying with a man when she clearly wanted to be with another. Jessie started for the door, but stopped in her tracks, spun around and faced her mother.

Angela Acosta looked older and wearier in the recliner by the window. *Why had she never seen how unhappy her mother was?* Maybe she hadn't wanted to look too hard.

"Does Hugh know about you and his father?"

"No. Jack has never told him. He wouldn't want Hugh to know the truth. Hugh looks up to his father. It would tear their family apart."

"This has been too much," Jessie said, shaking her head. "I'm leaving and I'm not sure when I'll be back. I need some time to digest this, and to make peace with everything you've laid in my lap and how I'm going to be able to live with myself keeping this from Daddy. Because you're right, knowing this would devastate him."

"Thank you."

"I know you told me all of this at great risk to your marriage and our relationship, but I have to tell you, Mama, I'm disappointed in you and I don't know if I'll ever get past this."

Tears trickled down her mother's cheek. "I know. And I understand. I wanted *you* to know that your future is your own."

As Jessie closed the door behind her, she planned on heeding her mother's advice and taking her future in her hands.

Starting now.

Ryan was ready for his second interview with Black Crescent. After spending the weekend with Ben, watching baseball and playing pool, Ryan felt positive about the day ahead. He'd left his brother's town house early, with enough time for the scenic drive into Falling Brook.

He arrived half an hour early for his interview and stared up at the notorious Black Crescent building. The angled roof, exposed concrete and wall of windows made it everything a modern midcentury office should look like. Parking his Porsche 911 Carrera, Ryan buttoned the jacket of his Armani suit as he walked inside.

A receptionist greeted him. "Good morning."

"Good morning. Ryan Hathaway to see Joshua Lowell."

"Yes, he's expecting you. You can take the elevator to the second floor." She motioned to the bank of elevators across from the desk. "They'll take you to Mr. Lowell's office."

"Thank you."

He followed her instructions, but when he stepped out of the elevator, no one was there to greet him. Instead, he found a tall, athletic man leaning over a large, circular desk. As he moved forward, Ryan caught sight of Haley Shaw, Joshua Lowell's assistant, sitting behind it. The man was murmuring something to her that Ryan couldn't hear, but Ryan suspected he was trying to come onto her. *Why else would he be looming over and in her personal space?*

"Is everything all right over here?" Ryan asked, moving forward. He glanced at Haley and then again at the man. He instantly recognized Chase Hargrove, one of the other candidates for the CEO position. Ryan had met him by accident at his first interview. "Perhaps you can give the lady some space?"

Chase's eyes narrowed and he rose to his full height. He was a few inches taller than Ryan, but Ryan didn't care. Ever since he was a kid and had been picked on, Ryan hated bullies. Once he'd gotten fit, Ryan vowed no one would ever take advantage of someone smaller or helpless again. It's why his Krav Maga classes were so important. This guy might outweigh him, but Ryan could take him down if needed.

"Everything is fine, Ryan," Haley said. "I've got this under control. Chase, make yourself scarce. I have work to do." Then she was sashaying down the corridor, leaving Ryan to follow behind her.

"Does he do that often?" Ryan asked, stepping in line beside her.

She grinned. "Yes, but he's harmless. No need for you to defend my honor. I'm a big girl. I can take care of myself."

"That's good to hear." Ryan stopped when she reached a closed door and knocked. When she heard the occupant's voice, Haley opened the door. "Mr. Lowell, Ryan Hathaway is here for his interview."

A pair of hazel eyes trained on Ryan as he entered the conference room "Ryan, thanks for coming in. Have a seat."

Haley closed the door behind her and took a seat next to Allison Randall.

The conference room was all glass with sleek, modern furniture done in muted gray and white. A large Sputnik chandelier hung over the table while the elongated acrylic back panels and white padded chairs were minimalist in their design. The man in the midst of it all, Joshua Lowell, looked the picture of a CEO today in what was no doubt an expensive charcoal suit and blue tie.

"Appreciate the invitation," Ryan said, taking a seat across from them.

"We've only extended the invite to a few candidates who I feel would be the best fit to lead this organization when I'm gone," Joshua said. "It's important I find someone who understands Black Crescent's history, so we're not destined to repeat the mistakes of the past."

"Understood," Ryan said. "And the strategies you've used for your investments have been traditional in the approach, but I do believe there are times some risks are worth taking. Like hiring the top talent in our industry to provide our clients with a more robust return while giving Black Crescent the management and performance fees."

"I'm eager to hear more," Joshua replied.

Over the next hour, Ryan discussed his ideas and vision for Black Crescent's future. When it was over, Joshua reached across the table and shook his hand. "You just might be exactly what this company needs."

Ryan chuckled softly. "I believe that's true and, if given the opportunity, I can show you what I can do. Is there anything in my qualifications that you see as lacking?"

"Your résumé is stellar. And you know that my only surprise is your willingness to leave behind a large Manhattan firm in favor of a small-town company like Black Crescent."

"Like you, I grew up here. My family is here. And I could see myself planting roots in Falling Brook."

Allison rose and walked Ryan to the door. "We'll be in touch, Ryan."

"I look forward to it."

Ryan marched out of the conference room full of swagger and feeling on top of the world.

He was nearly to his car when he unsilenced his phone and looked at his text messages.

Several were from his mother.

Hugh O'Malley is back in town.
Rumors say he's planning on proposing to Jessie.
Did you know?

Ryan's heart stopped. Now he knew why he hadn't heard from Jessie. She was here in Falling Brook. With Hugh. And ready to become a member of the O'Malley family. He was done with Jessie. He refused to allow her any more space in his head, but his heart was another matter entirely.

Opening the door, Ryan hopped inside, but once he did anger fueled him and he pummeled the steering wheel with his fists. Why couldn't Jessie have told him? Been honest and not let him believe what they'd shared was something special?

Well at least now he knew rather than hold out hope on something that would never be. What they'd shared was over. If he was lucky, Jessie would go back across the ocean with Hugh and he wouldn't ever have to see her again.

Would that hurt any less? Ryan doubted anything hurt this much. Because Jessie had just ripped his heart out and he would never be the same.

Sixteen

Ryan appreciated Adam allowing him to use the Hampton house for the night. He knew he was pouring salt in the wound by coming back to the scene of the crime, but there was a part of him that wanted to relive happier moments he'd spent with Jessie. He knew it was twisted, but he couldn't help himself. He certainly hadn't wanted to stay in Falling Brook to see Jessie and Hugh reunited. No thank you.

He would stay here and lick his wounds in the privacy of Adam's beach house. When Adam had asked if he wanted company, Ryan had declined. He needed time to think. Think about the direction of his life and figure out how he'd veered so far off course.

Getting involved with Jessie when she was not over Hugh had been an epic mistake, but looking back,

Ryan doubted he'd do things differently. The month he'd shared with Jessie had been exciting, thrilling and very *passionate*.

Sitting on the terrace, Ryan thought back to the night he'd looked out on this very same beach. He'd been wondering if he'd gotten his signals crossed when he'd kissed Jessie in that restaurant, but then he'd turned around and seen her silhouette in the moonlight as she'd stood at the doorway. He recalled sucking in his breath at the significance of the moment. He remembered what it had felt like to hold Jessie in his arms and to know she'd wanted him as much as he'd wanted her.

And she had.

For that one moment in time.

Ryan's cell phone rang, prompting him from his musing. The display read Joshua Lowell. He was surprised to hear from the CEO of Black Crescent directly, but instantly knew the reason for his call.

"Ryan Hathaway."

"Ryan, it's Joshua Lowell. Is now a good time? I was hoping we could talk."

"As good a time as any," Ryan responded.

"Excellent, well…" There was a pause on the other end of the line. "I wanted to call you personally and tell you that you made a quite an impression on me. You're exactly what Black Crescent needs, which is why I'm offering you the job of CEO. What do you say?"

Ryan inhaled. He'd wanted this position so badly and had worked hard his entire life to get to the point in his career to make this shift, but it didn't hold as much appeal as it once did. Being in Falling Brook wouldn't give him the distance he craved, not if Jessie was back with Hugh. Given how small the town was, Ryan would surely run into them and he couldn't stomach it. Why did she always go running back to Hugh when they not only lacked chemistry, which Ryan and Jessie had in abundance, but had absolutely nothing in common other than the fact that his father, Jack O'Malley, had helped her and Pete when they'd been younger. She didn't owe them her life, but Jessie *couldn't* or *wouldn't* see beyond the past. And so she was destined to repeat her mistakes.

Ryan was certain he was the only man who could truly make her happy. He'd never seen her as alive and vibrant as she'd been with him. And because he loved her, there was no way Ryan could take a job that would hurt Jessie and her family. Even though they weren't together, he couldn't do it. He owed her his loyalty if nothing else than for their twenty-year friendship.

"Ryan, are you there?" Joshua asked. "Did you hear me?"

"I did. And the answer is no. I can't accept the position."

After calling in sick to work, Jessie sat parked outside the Hathaway house for several seconds. She had no idea where Ryan was, but she had to find him. It wouldn't be easy. She'd put her and Ryan's relationship on pause while she'd *finally* dealt with her past. But she had and now she was ready to move forward with the man she loved.

Her call to Ryan went straight to voice mail, as had

the others all morning. She wasn't surprised. *Had she honestly expected him to pick up because she'd suddenly had an epiphany?* So she texted him. Again.

No response.

Damn.

She had to tell him she'd realized he was the only man for her, but she couldn't do that if he wouldn't pick up the phone. She had to tell him she'd made her peace and put Hugh and the past firmly behind her. Glancing up the driveway, she recognized Mrs. Hathaway's Audi and breathed a sigh of relief.

Jessie raced across the short distance, climbed the steps of the porch, pressed the doorbell and wrung her hands as she waited.

Marilyn Hathaway answered the door with a smile. "Jessie!" she cried. "What are you doing here?"

"I'm sorry to disturb you so late, Mrs. Hathaway, but I… I was hoping you'd heard from Ryan? I haven't been able to reach him and…" Her voice trailed off. She wasn't ready to spill her feelings to his mother on their front porch.

"Do you want to come in, dear?" his mother asked, but Jessie shook her head.

"No, ma'am. It's important that I find him. I have something to tell him."

"That you love him?" his mother asked quietly.

Had everyone realized her feelings before she had? "I…if and when I say the words, Mrs. Hathaway, they have to be to Ryan first."

"I completely understand, but I'm afraid I haven't heard from him. All I know is that he visited his brother

Ben this weekend before his interview this morning at Black Crescent."

So he was still pursuing the job? *That* stuck in Jessie's craw but they would have to figure it out somehow. She wouldn't let that dissuade her from speaking her truth, which was that she was madly, deeply, in love with him.

"Do you have Ben's number?" Jessie reached inside her purse and took out her iPhone, ready to dial him. "Perhaps I could speak with him?"

"Absolutely." Marilyn Hathaway pulled her phone from her back pocket and rattled the number off.

"Thank you so much." Jessie moved a few steps in and gave Ryan's mother a warm embrace. "You're a lifesaver."

"I wish you luck."

Jessie nodded. "I have a feeling I'm going to need it." She raced down the steps to her rental. Once inside, she called Ben immediately, but he wasn't much help, either. He informed her that Ryan was over being jerked around and had gone away to get some peace of mind from the roller coaster ride she'd taken him on. He also told her that he had no idea where Ryan had gone.

Jessie sat in the Hathaways' driveway, racking her mind on where Ryan could have gone to clear his head. She thought back over the last month and when Ryan had been his most happiest. And she knew where he would go.

It took her two hours to get to the Hamptons from Falling Brook, but Jessie was determined that this night wouldn't end without her telling Ryan how sorry she was for putting them through the paces. She would tell him how much she loved him and wanted a future with him.

But was she too late?

Would he even hear her out after she'd hurt him?

Thankfully, she had Tia's cell and after speaking with Adam, he'd given her the address to his Hampton beach house and even told her where to find a second spare key. Following the instructions Adam had so graciously given, after she'd promised him she was going to make amends with Ryan, she pulled up the gravel driveway. When she saw Ryan's Porsche 911 Carrera outside, she damn near wanted to weep with joy.

He was here.

She would get a chance to make things right. It would be the toughest sell of her life. Probably harder than any case she'd ever tried in mock court during law school, but Ryan was worth the fight.

Girding her loins, Jessie walked up the steps and found the planter that held the other key. Ryan would be out back on the terrace, watching the stars, with a beer.

She was right about the terrace.

But not the beer.

He was on the terrace, his eyes closed and head leaned back. He was wearing the same open shirt he'd worn that night she'd found him and had had the most exciting sexual encounter of her life. *Stop it. Focus.* That's when she saw a bottle of dark liquid sitting on the side table along with the empty tumbler beside it. Half the bottle was empty.

"Can I have one of those?" she asked softly.

Ryan jerked upright. When he saw her, he blinked several times as if to be sure she was really there. "You don't usually like dark liquor," he finally said.

"I feel like I need it."

He poured some from the bottle into his glass and handed it to Jessie.

She downed the two thumbs in one gulp, coughing slightly.

"That was meant to be sipped."

She shrugged. "Liquid courage."

"What the hell are you doing here, Jessie? The more important question is why." He raised an eyebrow. "I assume Adam told you where to find me?"

"Don't be mad at him. He was only trying to help."

"He should have stayed out of it."

Jessie ran her fingers through her hair. This was going to be more difficult than she'd thought. Ryan's eyes weren't glassy but they were cold as ice. It was like he was looking right through her.

"I'm sorry." She didn't know what else to say.

"Exactly what are you sorry about?" Ryan asked, folding his arms across his broad chest.

"For ignoring you this week. I was so conflicted about so many things and I needed time to figure it all out. It was wrong of me not to return your calls or texts."

"But you're not *conflicted* anymore?" He snorted.

She nodded. "That's right."

He threw back his head. "Really, Jessie? You figured this all out and it's back in a nice, neat box? Well, guess what, life isn't that easy."

"It is when you know what you want."

"And what's that?"

"You."

Seventeen

Ryan had waited a long time to hear those words. For Jessie to tell him it was *him* she wanted. That it was *him* she hungered for. But that time had come and gone. Sitting out here in the dark, he'd picked up the pieces of his heart that she'd crumbled.

He was never going to be the man she chose. He was always going to be second best. For his sanity and his pride, he'd accepted she was with Hugh O'Malley—and now she was here telling him exactly what he wanted to hear? It couldn't be. Clearly, he'd had too much to drink tonight.

"Don't lie to me, Jessie. It's cruel. What did you come here for? A roll in the hay? That's all I was good for the last month, so are you ready for a repeat? If so—"

he stood "—I think I can recreate our first escapade on this very same terrace."

"Stop it!" Jessie moved a few steps closer to him. "Don't do this, Ryan. Don't cheapen what we meant to each other. I mean, what we *mean* to each other."

"Me? I'm the one that's been fighting for us this entire time while you've been *conflicted, confused* or whatever other adjective you want to use. I've been very clear from day one *who* I wanted. And that was you. But you made it abundantly clear that you are with Hugh."

Jessie shook her head. "You're wrong. I'm not with Hugh. We broke up."

"Again?" Ryan laughed uproariously. "How many breaks is this now?"

"Stop being so pig-headed, Ryan. This wasn't a break. It was a breakup. I told my mom. And he told his parents. It's over. It has been for a long time. I think Hugh and I were content to have each other as a backup plan, but that's no way to live, and Hugh realized that, too."

"Bully for him." He reached for the bottle and poured himself another drink. "But what's that got to do with me?"

"Everything. Ryan, I'm bungling this, but what I'm trying to say, very badly, is that I love you."

Ryan's eyes blazed with anger. How dare she say those three words to him! "No, no." He pointed his finger at her while holding on to his glass. "So suddenly you're not with Hugh and you're running here to me because you love me? Do you honestly expect me to believe that?"

"Yes."

"Well, I don't. I don't believe you. Do you have any idea what you've done? I'm broken, Jessie. You broke me. You gave me everything I'd always wanted, allowing me to be with you, and then you snatched it all away in the next heartbeat."

"Ryan, please—" Jessie moved toward him, but he stepped away from her. He couldn't let her get any closer. It would be his undoing. He might falter and then where would he be? The sap who'd carried a torch for this woman for nearly two decades.

Ryan shook his head. "No way am I going to go through this again. I'm not giving my heart to you again and end up broken."

"I—I never meant to hurt you, Ryan. I thought I was doing what was right for me. For my family. You know I've felt beholden to the O'Malleys. They'd helped my family so much. Mr. O'Malley gave my mom a job, which ensured we were able to keep the house. It was because of him Pete and I had a future worth dreaming of. Staying with Hugh seemed like the right thing to do—to… you know, honor him, and thank him.

"Hugh was an O'Malley," she continued. "He was going places, which meant I would never end up nearly destitute like my father. It made sense on paper. But Hugh and I never had any sparks or passion between us. As the years went by, we grew further and further apart, but I was afraid to let go of the safety net he represented. So I stayed instead of opening myself up to the possibilities of what was right in front of me."

Ryan pointed to himself. "Are you talking about me?"

"Of course I am. The reaction I had to you on reunion night shook me to my core. It threw everything on its head about what I thought I wanted. Showed me I'd fooled myself into thinking love and passion didn't matter. And then we came here to the Hamptons and I could no longer deny the obvious. I wanted you. And the attraction was mutual and so hot, I wasn't ready for how powerful it was."

"Why are you telling me all this?" It hurt to hear and Ryan moved to the terrace sofa. His chest felt tight as he placed his drink on the table and took a seat.

"Because I need you to understand that I was mixed up about my family and Hugh, and it colored my thinking. But what I have never been confused about is you. I love you, Ryan. I fell in love right here—" she pointed downward to the deck "—in the Hamptons. I knew it wasn't just an affair, but I didn't really know what love was, so I didn't recognize it. Or maybe I was too afraid to, but I'm not anymore."

Jessie came forward and knelt in front of him. She took his hand in hers. "You're not second to Hugh, Ryan. You're second to none. You're the only man I want. I know I've been foolish for turning my back on the precious gift you gave me—your heart. But I promise you, if you give me another chance, a chance to make this right, I will show you in every way imaginable that I'm yours."

Ryan slid his hand out of hers and cupped her face. Jessie rested her face in his palm. She prayed she hadn't left it too late to tell him how much she loved him.

"I'm yours, too," Ryan stated. "I always have been,

Jessie. No other woman has ever, or will ever, measure up to you. You're it for me."

"Are you saying…?"

"I love you, Jessie."

She smiled through her tears and lowered her head. "Oh, thank God. I haven't lost you."

He lifted her chin and his brown eyes bore into her. "You haven't lost me, but I did try to forget you. I tried to tell myself not to love you, but I was fighting a losing battle. From the moment you stood inside the doorway of our tree house when you were six years old and asked me if you could come play, you've bewitched me and I've been yours ever since."

Jessie couldn't stop herself. She flung herself into his arms and he fell backward on the sofa. She sealed her lips against his and it was pure magic, sending the pit of her stomach free-falling into a wild swirl. She gave herself freely to Ryan because he was the only man she'd ever loved or ever would. There was a rightness in his kiss and it sang through her veins.

When his lips left hers to nibble at her earlobe, Jessie couldn't resist a low moan. When his lips returned to capture hers, he was more demanding. They kissed madly and deeply. It was wet and hot—so hot that Jessie surrendered any defenses she might have. Ryan took her weight, adjusting their position until she was sitting atop him and she could feel the press of his erection underneath her.

Jessie rocked her hips back and forth, teasing him, but it was her body that reacted swiftly and her inner thighs tightened around him in anticipation.

"If you keep doing that, I'm going to have to have you now."

"Go ahead," she murmured. "Have me." She lifted off him long enough for Ryan to reach underneath her dress and snatch the scrap of silk she'd been wearing. He tossed it on the deck. Then he was unbuttoning her shirt dress and pushing aside her bra. Jessie felt a gust of air on her nipple just before Ryan sucked it into his mouth. She shivered and moaned.

When he lifted his head, he stopped long enough to admire her breasts. "God, you're so beautiful."

"You make me feel beautiful." And he did. She felt like the sexiest woman alive in his arms.

"I don't have a condom."

"It's okay," Jessie slid one from the pocket of her dress.

"You naughty nymph." Once again, she'd come prepared to play.

Jessie grinned wickedly. "I hoped it wasn't the end of us. And I'm so glad I was right."

She helped him don the protection and then she guided him to where she wanted him. She impaled herself and rode him while Ryan sucked her nipples, taking his time to worship them with his mouth and tongue. Jessie melted into Ryan's hard chest and, though she wanted to ride him to swift peak, he was caressing her where they were joined.

He explored and incited her until a wave of pleasure so mighty and all-consuming engulfed Jessie and she broke while Ryan shouted his culmination. They tumbled back to earth, clinging to each other in the aftermath.

* * *

Ryan awoke with Jessie spooned tightly against him. Last night had been extremely gratifying and it was because they'd reinvented the Kama Sutra into the wee hours of the morning. They'd been so greedy for each other after a week apart, they'd stayed up half the night devouring one another. But eventually, he'd fallen into a peaceful sleep.

Awakening this morning, Ryan realized he had everything he could ever ask for. The woman he loved, loved him back. She'd *chased* after him, tracked him down to the Hamptons and revealed she was truly, madly, deeply in love with him. He couldn't ask for anything more. He'd wanted this for so long, for a moment he'd thought it had been a dream. But after closing his eyes tightly and reopening them, Jessie was still there wrapped in his arms.

It meant everything to him that Jessie made him a priority. It was a heady thought to think this beautiful, smart, independent woman was truly his. He stole a kiss, but when he did, her eyes popped open.

"Good morning," he said, glancing down at her sleep-deprived face.

"How long have I been asleep?" She rubbed the sleep from her eyes.

"Not long. I think I tired you out." He kissed the side of her neck then took her earlobe between his teeth. He reached for her breasts and they swelled in his hand.

"No fair, you know that's my sweet spot," she said breathily.

"Really? I thought this was…" He slid himself down

her body so his face was between her moist folds. Then he swiped his tongue back and forth.

"Oh God," she cried out, but Ryan continued sucking, prodding and kissing her intimately until shudders racked her body.

A few moments later, Ryan moved upward, utterly satisfied with his handiwork, and looked at Jessie. He liked seeing her satiated and completely uninhibited. He knew how lucky he was and he wasn't going to do anything to jeopardize what they'd built.

"I got the job with Black Crescent."

Jessie sat upright, pulling the sheet to cover her breasts. "I see." She nodded. "I know how important this is to you and that you need to do what you think is right. So I want you to know, I'll support you in whatever you decide."

"You will?" Ryan was taken aback. From the moment he'd mentioned it, Jessie had been dead set against his taking the job and he'd understood. Vernon Lowell's greed, and therefore Black Crescent, was the cause of her family's hurt and pain.

"Yes. Part of loving you is loving all of you, including what's important to you. And if you feel strongly that you can make a difference and turn the company around, then I'll stand by you."

"Jessie, you've no idea what this means to me, but I turned down the job offer."

Jessie's eyes grew bright with unshed tears. "You did?"

"I turned it down as soon as they made the offer last night."

"Last night? We weren't even together. Why would you do that?"

He gazed at her tenderly. "Because I will always put you first, Jessie, whether we're together or not."

Jessie caressed his cheek. "How did I ever get lucky enough to find you?"

He shrugged. "I don't know. Maybe thank your parents for moving next door?"

Jessie laughed at him. "I love you so much, Ryan. But I only want you to turn down this job offer with Black Crescent if you want to. I'd never want you to look back and resent me for holding you back from your dreams."

"You're my dream," Ryan stated swiftly. "And I don't want to spend another moment apart from you." He lowered himself to the floor by the bed in front of her.

"What are you doing?" Jessie asked, clutching the sheet to her chest.

Ryan knelt on one knee and reached for her hand. "Jessie Acosta. I have loved you since I was six years old. I love your beauty, spirit and passion and there's no one else in the world for me, but you. Will you do me the honor of being my wife?"

"Yes, yes!" Jessie leaped into his arms and Ryan fell backward onto the floor, taking Jessie with him. "I love you, and I can't wait to be Mrs. Ryan Hathaway."

Epilogue

"Welcome to the fold," Marilyn Hathaway told Jessie when she and Ryan arrived at the Hathaways' annual July Fourth barbecue the following year.

She and Ryan had been married three weeks ago. It had been a small, intimate ceremony on the beach at Adam's Hampton house. His best friend had not only allowed them use of the house for the wedding, but had stood as Ryan's best man. Jessie's bestie, Becca, had been her maid of honor. Both Ryan and Jessie's parents had been in attendance. They'd only recently come back from honeymooning in Hawaii.

Ryan had booked them a villa with an infinity pool and stunning lagoon. Most of their time had been spent making love in the palatial master bedroom. Though they had, eventually, ventured out into the resort to eat delicious tropical meals, drink wine, swim in the pool or snorkel in the ocean.

"Thank you, Mom," Jessie said, responding to his mother before she departed to tend to other guests. Marilyn Hathaway had refused to allow her to call her anything else and Jessie didn't mind it one bit, especially since she wasn't close with her mother at the moment.

Since her mother's revelation of her long-standing affair with Jack O'Malley, their relationship had been strained. It was hard for Jessie to come home knowing everything she'd ever believed was a lie. She did visit, but they usually stayed with the Hathaways to avoid any awkwardness. If her father had noticed, he'd never said anything. Jessie suspected he knew something was wrong between her and her mother, but he didn't pry.

Jessie was thankful because, although she didn't agree with her mother's behavior, she refused to be the person who broke up their marriage and forced her father out of the only home he'd ever had. And so she'd kept her mouth shut. Though her mother had recently shared with Jessie that she'd ended her affair with Jack O'Malley, much to his chagrin, Jessie didn't know whether she had done it for Jessie or for herself. Regardless, she'd taken her at her word that it was over.

"Is everything okay, babe?" Ryan said from her side. "You looked like you were somewhere else."

"I'm sorry. I zoned out for a minute." Jessie shook her head, trying to shake off any negative vibes. Today was a day for enjoying her new family—and, besides, there was one more in the Hathaway clan now. Monica, Ryan's older brother Sean's wife, had had a baby girl a couple of months ago, and everyone in the family was excited and fawning over the newest addition. The seven-pound baby was a pure delight.

It made Jessie want to make some babies of her own with Ryan someday, but only after they had a couple of years to enjoy each other.

"Well, whatever is troubling you, you know you can talk to me, right?" Ryan whispered.

"I know." And she did, Ryan had always been her rock. That would never change. In fact, Jessie would say their connection was stronger because he was her husband. She knew he would protect her and vice versa. On the beach in the Hamptons, when she'd said her vows to love, honor and protect him, she'd meant them.

"Good, so let's join the family. I think everyone's ready for a game of charades."

"Sounds like fun."

Jessie grabbed his hand as he led her toward her new future; a fulfilling life with a loving husband and his family. It was a life she hadn't known she wanted, but now that it was here, Jessie couldn't think of any place she would rather be.

* * * * *

Dynasties:
Seven Sins

It takes the betrayal of only one man
to destroy generations.
When a hedge fund hotshot vanishes with billions, the
high-powered families of Falling Brook
are changed forever.

Now seven heirs, shaped by his betrayal,
must reckon with the sins of the past.

Passion may be their only path to redemption.

Experience all Seven Sins!

Ruthless Pride *by Naima Simone*
Forbidden Lust *by Karen Booth*
Insatiable Hunger *by Yahrah St. John*
Hidden Ambition *by Jules Bennett*
Reckless Envy *by Joss Wood*
Untamed Passion *by Cat Schield*
Slow Burn *by Janice Maynard*

Available May through November 2020!